M000208842

Air of Solitude

THE SWISS LIST

GUSTAVE ROUD

Air of Solitude

FOLLOWED BY

Requiem

TRANSLATED BY
SEAN T. REYNOLDS AND ALEXANDER DICKOW

LONDON NEW YORK CALCUTTA

swiss arts council
prɔhelvetia

The publication has been supported by a grant
from Pro Helvetia, Swiss Arts Council

Seagull Books, 2020

Gustave Roud, A*ir de la solitude*
© Association des Amis de Gustave Roud

Gustave Roud, *Requiem*
© Association des Amis de Gustave Roud

First published in English translation by Seagull Books, 2020
English translation © Sean T. Reynolds and Alexander Dickow, 2020

The translations of 'Difference' and 'Prairie's Powers' first appeared
in the journals *Plume* and *Calque*, respectively.

ISBN   978 0 8574 2 687 1

British Library Cataloguing-in-Publication Data
A catalogue record for this book is available from the British Library

Typeset by Seagull Books, Calcutta, India
Printed and bound by WordsWorth India, New Delhi, India

CONTENTS

115

Requiem

A FOREWORD BY ANTONIO RODRIGUEZ

According to the legend common since his death, Gustave Roud (1897–1976) was the reflection of the character who wanders through his lyrical prose, the transparent double of the 'poet' described in his books. As a figure isolated in his Swiss village, in his 'air of solitude', he supposedly maintained ties only through correspondence, a few rare visits from friends, walking in the plains, and writing: 'Come. No one is here. I am alone with the birds.' His poetry would thus have an autobiographical basis, almost documentary in relation to the 'remote countrysides'. Little inclined to travel or to develop an imagination of the exotic, his poetry's spiritual impact is rooted in his landscape in order to flush out the 'scattered features' of a profane Eden— following Novalis' injunction, for henceforth 'Paradise is dispersed throughout the earth.' The legend of

Gustave Roud might therefore summon forth, in an entirely different context, the figure of Emily Dickinson, calling upon the ideal of a life of secular withdrawal from the world, entirely dedicated to poetry, by a discreet man inhabited by a fire as humble as it is sacred. One of Dickinson's poems might indeed sum up the legend constructed around Roud:

> Our lives are Swiss,—
> So still, so cool,
>   Till, some odd afternoon,
> The Alps neglect their curtains,
> And we look farther on.

> Italy stands the other side,
> While, like a guard between,
> The solemn Alps,
> The siren Alps,
> Forever intervene!

For him, it is not the Alps that intervene but a 'windowpane unbreakable and pure', authorizing the fleeting glance *elsewhere*, yet not granting access to that imagined Italy: 'How our hands resemble one another! How easy it is to speak to men, how little then do they ask to recognize you! For I am one of you, am I not?' (p. 89) Roud made all of French-speaking Switzerland dream poetically upon itself, the land that welcomed European Romanticism from Rousseau to Byron, from Lamartine to Shelley. His poetry could seem idyllic, sustained by an ethereal figure of constantly conflicted desires (more or less unspeakable, always displayed), and a moral, sacrificial figure inspired above all by Novalis and Hölderlin. The legend does not prove completely false, but it remains terribly biased and incomplete, and leaves us relating to his work and trajectory in a much more lacklustre way than the breadth and embodiment of his project allows. Since the year in Switzerland consecrated to his work in 2015, reading Roud has been altered by critical work led by the University of Lausanne,[1] and these new readings, more open and more charged than before, can henceforth be undertaken in different languages. This English translation gives us the opportunity to discover his intoxicating and pure world in a new way.

Also, we must speak of the wild desire of his work, of its necessity before life, no longer simply hinting at it at the edge of conversation, hardly daring to call it a 'difference' without recognizing in it the central theme and impetus of his aesthetic. The whole work is built on difference and the search for affinity. Let us not reduce such a deviation to mere homoerotic orientations, for this 'difference' is larger in scope: it concerns family legacy, religious practice, political commitments. And this threshold provides the dynamics of a celebration of daily life through imagination, and of the will to link men through rhythm. We are not re-establishing the legend, to the extent that Roud, in his life as in his work, inaugurates a gesture that is a great deal more embodied, more overflowing, more excessive especially, than the usual image would have it. He gazes fixedly at his Italy, an Italy of sharing and purity: 'Yet one day I did discover that there was *another* purity, that of human innocence. / I was saved by a glance' (p. 98). It is not the spirit, the idea or abstract beauty that sustain purity but the human gaze, eyes that cross paths and understand one another. The lyrical scope of his writing leads him to deploy the embodied forms of an intense experience of reality: the flash of an instant allows for the rediscovery of an order in the world's chaos. His poetry thinks, but not intellectually or abstractly; it thinks outward from the changing imagination of its time: between self-destruction and reconstruction, between roots and movement, between spiritual progress and rural primitivism. His work incorporates a reverie and an aesthetic of tension, just as his life is made of numerous insurmountable paradoxes hardly containable in the image of the poet-recluse.

A sensitive man, highly educated, Roud remained a tireless walker, going out to meet others, sometimes playing on a certain distinction proper to the man of letters or the landowner, escaping from the farmer's cycle yet magnifying it aesthetically. His body of work is built on the terrible divide between the attachment to the surrounding land and an aesthetic detachment from rural custom, between a desire for masculine bodies and an art which articulates their parts, their

Antonio Rodriguez

limits, towards an indefinite space of exchange. Thus, the description of landscapes and farmers, who are the human extension of the landscape, offers up a quest for a 'poetic place' in which the energies of the body and the spirit confront, combine, liberate one another. The landscape becomes body while the body becomes landscape, like that 'valley where I advanced among the invisible shoulder-blows of the wind' (p. 46).

In contact with the principal Swiss publishers, Roud became, after the war, an unavoidable figure for the young poets of French-speaking Switzerland, who came to him and even climbed up to the village of Carrouge to receive his recognition: this was the case for Philippe Jaccottet, Jacques Chessex, Maurice Chappaz and the main poets of this part of Switzerland, a land of poetry. Amid the countryside of the Vaud, Roud's literary aesthetic magnified his passion for the bodies of the peasants through a poetic prose as ardent as it is restrained, seeking a 'human paradise,' influenced by Rimbaud, Claudel and the Greek ideal. It turned away from Lake Léman and the Alps, so celebrated by the Swiss master of the period, C. F. Ramuz. As a photographer, the *modus operandi* of his perspectives, ample and controlled, unfolded across 50 years, with a surprising feel for experimental technique, and a European if not world aesthetic of the athlete (the athlete of the fields) tied to, but also in contrast with his poetry, which is more marked by a certain aestheticism.

The books translated here are those of the mature writer, turning away from desire to more radical explorations of death. They are written in poetic prose with a particularly rhythmic and supple syntax, thus following Mallarmé's legacy as opposed to Surrealism or the first minimalists. If Roud wrote some verse, it remains less intense than his prose. One must read his prose as the starting point of a body of work now in the process of being collected, work of great variety, as indicated, for example, by the monographic website devoted to him.[2] His poetic prose has the density of a core nestled within layer upon layer. Thus, the writing of *Requiem*, for instance, took several decades; the author writes texts, reworks them, sometimes publishes a part of them, assembles them, removes parts of them. Such a writing dynamic excites adepts of manuscripts and critical editions, but it might quite simply impress any reader: these texts, so assured, so polished by time, are far from being totally stabilized prose works; they remain in motion, in formation, in search of themselves and of the dream of an even more ideal poetry. Besides an extremely elaborate syntax, Roud likes to make his language ring out as he depicts sublime rural tableaux. We thus find a country totally transformed poetically, in which everyday activities become the gestures of a possible harmony with the world always threatened by smallness, solitude, confinement: 'Long ago I held the belief for many years that winter, in separating him from the world, restores man to himself' (p. 50).

Antonio Rodriguez

In *Requiem* (1967), the countryside assumes a new substance in search for the dead mother. Always, Roud's prose has sought to reconcile opposites, to overcome that which was divided, to the extent that all distance becomes for him an irresistible call. His mother's death led him to constitute a poetic whole through time, across more than 30 years, not without the encouragement of his friends who saw him grow weak in the last years of his life, who saw him doubt his gestures more and more yet persevere. This dialogue with his mother is built also with what remains alive in him and in men, an intense search for harmony with that which should be in harmony, as well as a crossing of time between moment and memory, between ephemeral and eternal: 'Already (but this word outside of time just died) from the most faraway region of the chasm an echo struggles to answer, more fragile than a young sprout out of the loam of silence, in the light of eternity' (p. 151).

It would be possible for us to replay the legend, to prop it up. Yet we will not renew it, not only because Carrouge is not Amherst but also because the significance and intensity of his work is revealed to be more important in its thrust. If desire in the landscape, photography, exchanges with other homosexual writers have interested me so much, it is neither out of a taste for scandal nor for personal reasons but because the very aesthetic project of this author seemed to me suddenly to reach a new magnitude, European, transnational, transmedial, and no longer regional, identitarian, by way of a bit of poetic prose. His translation into English participates in this burgeoning. His poetry, the few volumes translated here, which form the centre of his work, seemed to me to display a greater scope. When I began to write about him, I was myself in part caught up in the established vision of him, without realizing that it was to a large extent a construction built up by a great Swiss poet, Philippe Jaccottet, who developed, as Roud's principal inheritor, the figure of his master.[3] He forged and superbly consolidated the legend which placed him in the wake of Novalis, Hölderlin, Rilke, in a genealogy of modernized Romantic poetry. Other voices indicated other paths, but they were hardly heard before the 2010s, which were a moment of rediscovery of the works' heterogeneity and scope, or of his abundant activity as a photographer. Many may thus partake in the 'poetic place' masterfully constructed by Roud; it becomes more than a mere poeticized testimony of its time and immediate space. Make no mistake, Roud built along the path of simplicity a work lofty and complex, between literature and photography, at the heart of Europe between the two World Wars. This work everywhere resonates today, and continues to inspire lively enthusiasm in younger generations of writers and readers.

Antonio Rodriguez

Notes

1   The catalogue of the Year of Gustave Roud 2015 provides new readings of the poet's work beyond the legends: Philippe Kaenel and Daniel Maggetti (eds), *Gustave Roud: la plume et le regard* (Gollion: Infolio, 2015).

2   This is the monographic site that has allowed different facets of the writer to be shown before the publication of his complete works, in progress: http://www.gustave-roud.ch.

3   Claire Jaquier, Daniel Maggetti and Antonio Rodriguez, (eds), *Les Cahiers Gustave Roud* (special issue 'Gustave Roud et Philippe Jaccottet: quelle filiation littéraire?') 15 (2014).

Air of Solitude

TRANSLATED BY SEAN T. REYNOLDS

AND ALEXANDER DICKOW

Prayer for a Stain upon the Eyes

Speak aloud the name of the person and say: *If you have the stain the Lord unstains you if it is white let it be unwhitened if it is red let it be unreddened if it is black let it be unblackened in the name of the Father and of the Son and of the Holy Spirit amen.*

Say this three times over and blow into the eye.

Presences at Port-des-Prés

The very high barn among the prairies, with its freshly tiled roof where the skies of summer brighten, the pebbledash walls, the bench forever empty between two closed doors, this Port-des-Prés is quite the same (it would seem) as other barns in other prairies and thus I return to it ceaselessly, as if, outside the sands of the real, miraculously an oasis was given to me where the absolute power of the heart might triumph in the end?

I crossed September fields, I greeted farmers sowing their rye, the first sowers of wheat. One worker was yawning in the sun, stretching out giant tanned arms against the hills, a village at each fist. The path teetered like a boat through the swaying landscape, abandoned to the winds, to the clouds, bizarrely battered by dull waves of shadow. Another worker talked to me as though he were talking in his sleep, in a rushed and frenzied voice—the voice of my lost friend. Perhaps it was him, since Port-des-Prés was quite near to where Time would soon go to lose its power . . . Here is the bench where I sit down without disrupting the greeting of the birds: the black redstart, the finch fallen from the roof, a chickadee scratches the dust with its many tiny claws. The fountain sings and loses its breath at each assault of the wind. There is yet another voice, that of the stream beneath the ash trees like a deep monotone incantation. Time falls asleep. O presences, what therefore impedes your appearance?

This man who's short of breath, black-lipped, with his cane and little box full of strangled beasts, he's the one who was found hanging in his barn one night in late autumn . . .

—Sit down. Don't be afraid. As you can see, no one is here. Good hunt? It is hard, indeed, when the heart falters at every step. They left the bench behind? Of course, why would they have taken it away? They sit back down there at hay season, into harvest time; they drink their 'four o'clock' coffee there, just as they once did between two carts of hay. Remember, and how those women laughed to see you wearing one of their big harvesting hats! But you, you were no longer laughing, already weary by work too heavy for your weakened arms. One final time you helped my friend, that autumn day when he was working alone with his spirited horses. You knew you were, so to speak, 'obliged'. And little by little this reprieve turned dreadful . . . Look around, nothing changes here, since they boarded up your house on the slope of the ravine. The same fountain—with a bit more moss in the basin. All the apple trees are there, their crowns a bit more ample, just barely. No, don't be frightened, that's the sound of the cart. The boy will not even see you, poor man. Rest just as you were when we had been speaking without haste, our rakes leant against the wall, and I still have so many things I wanted to ask you, to tell you ... He *can't* see us, I promise you. Tell me, ans—

The cart passes and I'm alone again.

Then, almost immediately, it's you. How you come back to life, how in a leap you settle into your violent purity. Just a moment ago you were merely the rustle of flowers and grass, a vague body the leaves blew through, and your scythe slid down the basin without a spark. Yet already your true man's lips are breaking the arm of glistening water, two arms of flesh dip up to the shoulder in the cool freshness. A shadow is restored to you. It's panting at your heels like a dog, stumbling over its heavy stones icy with sky. You wipe your lips with the back of your hand. You look at me without smiling, sullen and weary of the teetering dancers of dawn, eyelids scorched, in the wine-red new day. Fatigue cuts you down at my side in a single stroke. Quick, before you sleep, before you depart again to your eternal harvests, open your eyes once more and look! Nothing has changed, has it? Up there is the village where you lived, the same one, that first rooftop past the orchards, beneath the four heaven-bearing poplars. And so close, at the tip of the furrow, the plough that you'll recognize.

Gustave Roud

You *must* live here on my embrace, on my anticipation. Help me. I won't always be so strong. What shall I do, that day when I see your hands fading again, one and then the other, to transparency, the day when wind blows out the flame of your voice? What shall I become if this place, the only place where my solitude is still refuted, this reef outside time where frightened presences plummet, falter, brought down from intemporal skies by a call of the heart, you abandon it forever? Already your life is no longer faithful to the *other* life. You did not sleep thus, open-handed, without a bat of your lashes. The trace of your dark hair against the chalk wall slowly grows paler. Your arm grows tarnished. The other arm. The little ring of faded silver passes through a misty finger and falls. You—

An empty bench.

A scent now unfurls its strange waves of honey and engulfs me. It is Time who dispatches this insidious harbinger of its presence. How well it has known what to choose! The aroma wherein the sap of man and plant mysteriously unite, who could better attach once more the absent culprit to plants, to men, at the close of the season, even in the last hour? No need to turn my eyes to the fields: I suddenly *feel* the September sun upon this already wilted morning; with closed eye I see a horse abruptly lift its head, tearing off windrows of tufts from tender stalks, the boys stabbing the mown clover with a tired pitchfork. I *know* they laugh, how you used to laugh, a summer flower blooming in the lip's blood, the same flower . . . No, I will not join them: there will always be *time*. O that a little rest should yet be given to me upon this thin bench of coarse wood, this vain bridge between two worlds, this shoreline beaten in turns by time and eternity! Let me remain immobile, ear open to this double abyss, a hand outstretched to those who *know* and who, by a single beat of our hearts, are wrested from the eternal, while the other searches in vain beneath the temporal swell, like a blind diver, looking to seize those who call themselves the *living*. Let the living mock the hand outstretched to the dead, mock all the presences that I welcome here until the hour when their too-*sure* footsteps frighten them away! Perhaps one day, haunted by the anxious call of these lipless voices, one of them will come to sit by my side. I will tell him what I *know*, with the simplest words. We will wait, as I wait each day, my back bruised by the wall, my feet in the dust covered with hay and bird tracks. And together we will finally see what I *have seen*: the unspeakable instant of ecstasy when time stops, when the road, the trees, the river, all is seized by eternity. The ineffable suspense! . . . The dead around us, the immobile sun as if forever at the tip of an oak, a bare leaf beneath our eyes that bursts with light, eternal, the voices inside a silence more peopled than our hearts, a solemn rumbling music in the veins of the world like blood. Not peace: a foundational stirring, from marrow

8

Gustave Roud

to clasped hands, and the oppressive, the vertiginous welling up of tears . . .

These tears, our response in the end to those of the thousands of obstinate angels who call to us and besiege us, according to the Voyant and his irrefutable voice:

. . . *the truth, which may encircle us with its weeping angels!*

Night falls very quickly. Aimé leaves early in the morning to the clover fields. The sun sets in a sky so pure that the moment appears as if suspended: one forgets the furtive work of the shadow. And yet it climbs ceaselessly, it seems to well up imperceptibly from the earth and drown it little by little, like a marsh engorged on water. We walk part of the night, we sink slowly into the darkness. The last clover falls, it's a sliver of night that falls into the greater night; the scythe is an invisible whistling right up to the instant that Aimé lifts it upright and sharpens it: a hand of night caresses a pale steel crescent against the sky. The villages one by one branch out, human constellations that will blaze out as the others do, into the dawn. Let's go, it is time to make our way back towards our lamps, to rummage through the icy dew and the prairie—but while we are yet one voice and one voice, and barely two traces (which are our faces), allow that I might say a kind of goodbye to what just vanished, like a sound among the other sounds of twilight, and which will no more be reborn this year: your last stroke of the sickle.

Extreme Autumn

How quickly it goes indeed, the gliding of one moribund season into the season to come! Still yesterday
(it seems like yesterday), this great land beneath a
searing September sun was surrendering to the ploughs.
Through the prairies of short grass, they opened up long
rose wounds that widened by the hour. At the tip of the
last furrow, Fernand, his shoulder bare and golden as in
the fullness of summer, one hand upon the glistening
ploughshare, the other lifting to his lips an apple so red
that the sky around it awoke its too-gentle blues. During
their break, the weary horses fell asleep and their manes,
leaning into slumber, unveiled in slivers a ribbon of
horizon, its hillsides, its tiny, delicately drawn villages,
with the precise account of rooftops and trees, its
colours posed side-by-side without a single flaw, barely
dulled across leagues of air matured like golden wine.

(Yes, this imperceptible pink bouquet, there at the
edge of the sky, it was Villars-le-Comte—but do we dare
to say it now that the villages have lost their names and
the headless stalks of the signposts sadly announce this

break with baptism? What does it matter, let us repeat it in a low voice, this beautiful name that paints the interval so well, the protraction of a row of scorching houses along the northward road, one by one—and then the meadows start up again and soon thereafter the tall ice-glazed forests ... Another year we will go up there, won't you, and you will see it as I have seen it, lying on the edge of a valley of ripe harvests, leaning on this deep cut of blue and yellow where the morning wind mixes the scent of blooming clover and hot hay, the living shadows and the glint of the scythes, the clocks and the cries. And you will come to know other villages, Neyruz, Denezy, Vuissens and its thin church like a gold pencil, the muted carpet of flowers that its young girls arrange for the Corpus Christi procession. And this pale grey mark, at mid-hill, that's Foulaverney, my great-grandfather's house and that of his sons, a great leaning structure I once visited, a knot in my heart, trying in vain to link to my presence the stories of the last century: the never-ending harvests, the village markets we went down to each week, and the August day when we brought back over nine hundred bundles.)

The land of sowing and, for many weeks, the land of bells. Every morning, the river of loud herds follows the roads' bed, leaves its banks and slowly submerges the countryside. Occasionally, the sky changes and becomes populated by impalpable herds, clouds or vapours with the wind as sole shepherd. The shadow of these celestial cattle glides haphazardly above the flocks

Gustave Roud

of the earth. The shepherd Robert no longer recognizes his beasts beneath the billowing cloaks of night and day. Shepherd Robert, summer's companion, how long it has been since the days when, under the imperfect shade of the cherry tree, your master poured us the rose wine of the nine o'clock break! You held in your fist, firm against your even darker chest, the dark loaf of bread to cut in thick slices, the first rose of June tucked beneath your hatband. And now here you are standing in your old earth-coloured clothes, your face and hands flushed by the north wind and the bitter green of trampled grass, a whip within your numb fingers . . . Over there, in the nearly deserted orchards, the last apples are shaken down, these sweet little apples that will be mashed. The tree trembles, the hail of fruit hammers the grass with a sound recognizable among a thousand others, a brief beat of a muffled drum, and the slanting swarm of leaves hesitates and alights as a flock of birds. Already the hidden man is about to come back down, searching with his blind slipper for the favourable branches. A small girl kneels near the baskets and coughs. This shiver of late afternoons, ah! how it grabs hold of the body and, more surely still, the heart! Then, suddenly, two nights of snow consummate the sacrifice of the leaves. The step near the mill disturbs the black and rimed hide of the ash trees. The willow on the canal, turned blonde like a mane, lets down its rain of leaves so gently that the still water barely trembles . . . In the countryside given over to silence, without labourers, without hunters, without flocks, rises and falls, like a lament taken up a hundred times over, the long complaint of the threshing machines. Tall carts of dead sheaves are seen passing on the road, like a summer treasure turned to cinder beneath the powerless sun. And there, rising from the valley, in great pale and furtive waves where the landscape silently unravels, hill after hill, village after village, tillage after tillage, the devourer of lamps and stars, the treacherous lord of late autumn, the fog.

A small rain sizzles, then stops abruptly. Little by little the blood withdraws from these moribund villages I leave behind one after the other with no regrets.

A few dragoons pass, then others, seeming lost—happy to be lost. They have a white canvas band around their helmets, small, rosy, innocent faces beneath the wing of painted steel. They prudently inquire as to the presence of officers. There instantly is the innkeeper on the front step, pouring them a wine as gold as the leaves.

Letter

For Henry-Louis Mermod

Two wheat carts: the very wee hours of a thresher's morning.

For it is not yet the time of long days spent threshing until nightfall. The wheat for sowing, ten or so big sacks perhaps, that is what we need for the moment, and nothing more.

Two wheat carts, but the best of the harvest, the part left standing till the hour of the scythe, the part where the hay is tallest, the ears heaviest. (I recall this field on the hill, from very far off quite the same as a tawny sand-bank against which the blue sky would break, a blue riven with violet and rose and which took on, at the touch of this ripening harvest, a sort of earthly weight. What a fire on the three mowers in the scent of hot hay and clover fading! Before me Fernand halts, sets his scythe upright and sharpens it. The sun, like an oil-soaked finger, draws and discloses upon the broad naked back the play of muscles, that lovely secret keyboard of a young body about to reach the height of its powers . . .)

Two wheat carts that carried with them into the barns' blackness the humming blaze of summer, two carts that we stacked again yesterday, sheaf upon sheaf, with pitchforks, and led to the threshing machine by a path of puddles and dying leaves, past ploughing and waterlogged prairies. Nothing more sorrowful than these carts of a harvest arisen again in the miserly light of October or November. It seems to have followed, inside its prison of beams and shingles, the slow decline of the season itself. The pale hay of the long, weary sheaves matches the worn-out day. Fernand (the harvester of old), his fist at the head of his horses, would turn towards me, beneath the flap of grey felt, a barely gilded face, and the blue of his gaze become like that of the mountains there above the valley, elusive and soft.

*

Where did I get this persistent love for great solitary farms lost amid their orchards and their prairies, closed universes, the sole places in the world where Sundays yet keep the taste of true Sundays, where one might sometimes find that thing more and more wrested from man: rest. From a childhood spent in one of these houses? Perhaps. I do not know, just as I am ignorant also from whence is born my contentment at living a few hours in one of those mills that are still found here and there in our countryside, in the fold of a river or a stream. They have a wheel (or no longer have it) day by day mossier, and drowse near their lock where the dragoons in summer come to bathe their naked horses. There, a bit of flour is made (not much), autumn fruit is crushed, poppies and walnuts are pressed, the harvest is sometimes threshed. There are many birds in the willows and the alders and fishermen often on the shore, never weary of being patient in vain. Also places where rest dwells. Could drama happen there? Could the 'young blond-haired valet miller' of the *Beautiful Miller's Daughter* lie down in the water for ever and the river sing him that lullaby that is still sung because of Schubert and which is already, without music, entirely music:

> *Good rest, good rest . . .*
> *Close your eyes!*
> *Weary wanderer, here is your home welcoming you . . .*
> *I prepared for you*
> *The cool bed, the tender pillow*
> *In the blue crystal's heart in my little chamber.*
> *Come here, come here*
> *What cradles and sways!*
> *Cradle to sleep, cradle the boy to sleep . . .* *

No, don't you think? And yet I remember my astonishment long ago, reading these poems. They could have been composed *right here*, on this bridge that our two carts of wheat crossed yesterday with the creaking of

---

* Adapted according to Roud's variations from Berton Coffin, Werner Singer and Pierre Delattre, *Word-by-Word Translations of Songs and Arias*, VOL. I (Oxford: Scarecrow Press, 1966), p. 369.

brakes overtightened, then loosened, on this bridge
where I can effortlessly see a Müller in a romantic cape
leaning, tilting his too-pink face framed with sideburns
and blond curls, perhaps to throw in a final farewell to
his ill-fated hero or to catch on the shore the gaze of a
flower that, like all true poets, he knows how to read.

*

Separated from the mill by a garden that is a solemn procession of particoloured dahlias, by the road and a space
of enclosed pastures and meadows, the threshing
machine occupies a barn and is arranged in three tiers.
All the way at the top where we have stacked our
sheaves gape the jaws of the machine, the metal-toothed
drum into which, from the table where the miller himself spreads it out, the raw wheat slides towards the
divorce of hay and grain. There are a few steps to descend,
and one arrives in a little room open to the north onto
an overhanging cement walkway. That is where the
sifted hay falls and piles up. Caught in a moving web of
brown string and blue cast-iron hooks, the hay turns
back into bundles (vain bundles). Lined up against the
sidewalk, an empty cart receives them, and one last time
the trembling castle of hay is built. Beneath this chamber of bundles, at the heart of a low room taking on daylight over the rumbling water and foliage, in a pretty
tumult of ventilators and belts, the pure grain separates
from the chaff and flows into three sacks hanging next
to each other (the last one for the small grain); two other

sacks, beneath the belly of the machine, receive the chaff . . . And the chaff sprays out in light swirls, falls back onto a stretched-out floorcloth, raising pretentious pyramids dispersed with a flick of the hand.

This bagging room is my residence for the morning. Perhaps Fernand granted it to me for friendship's sake, guessing what pleasure I might take in a few gestures and, still more, in gliding through my hands, as from a spring, the wheat's inexhaustible jet. There is no longer, as at the threshing machines of times past, that plentiful presence of dust that made our fellow labourers cough, spit and swear all at once. We barely saw each other through a sort of perpetual rain of ash, a threat of night that disappeared only with the real night. Nothing affronts the length of landscape I am contemplating, and I can cinch and shake the full sacks, hang up the empty ones (with their naive stencilled bouquets, their names half worn away, in that lovely writing of times past, forever vanished), tie the floorcloths bursting with chaff without the slightest blasphemy. The very sound of the threshing machine, a lament without pathos, does not interrupt thought but rather sharpens it with an edge of fatigue that is also a kind of intoxication. Contrary to a train inscribing in the brain the naked rhythm in which some errant melody becomes mercilessly stuck, or to a stream that haunts you deliciously with a thousand mingled voices: reflections of phrases, reflux of songs, the lamentation of threshing lodges itself right away in the ear, once and for all, embeds itself in the mind, weaving a sort of neutral background against which stand out reveries, gazes, other sounds, even victorious ones over this basso continuo: up to this limpid, this aching birdsong.

(Three full sacks, and I can tie the first floorcloth beneath a prickly rain of glumes.)

Without the monotonous succession of filled and empty sacks, I would live here outside of time. And I need only turn my eyes towards the bit of landscape granted me to return to a sort of absolute. It is the time of 'grey weather' dear to painters concerned with ripping objects and beings out of the moment in order to place them in their eternity. The light neither grows nor fades. A steady daylight bathes all things: the grass at my threshold green in its *true* everlasting green, the stream swollen with the rains precipitating its eternal disorder, the eternal wagtails on the shore (not those of the ploughing but those of the streams, larger, with a pretty green-and-yellow breast), the eternal hedge of alders and ash trees whose tops a light fog comes to gnaw at . . . Fernand himself, who has left his horses to say farewell to me, and who leans back against the wall, his palm full of wheat that he tastes a grain at a time, Fernand becomes, with all his serene strength half-unaware of itself, this young eternal peasant, as my long quests once glimpsed him from village to village. I am surrounded by essential presences; it seems that all is ready for the heart to find its satisfaction, for our profound hunger for poetry to be finally appeased . . .

An abrupt return of memory seizes me by the throat and all collapses into anguish.

*

I owed you the confession of this collapse, dear friend. Forgive me the interminable story that precedes it, and that was there only to make felt, by contrast, the suddenness, the unpredictability of this sort of *ruination*. I remember that at that moment I took your letter from a pocket of my overalls (where it was lodging between a bunch of twine and the slice of bread for the 'nine o'clock'). I reread your words: *The war creates a present that we did not choose. Beyond the civic and charitable obligations it imposes on us, it gives us plenty of leisure to flee into poetry; the war that threatens our life threatens what we love the most in life: poetry. Poets thus take on a singular topicality, for never will we have read them with more fervour.* That's clear indeed, and exact. But you speak of the poetry that we read, hence of a poetry that is *already made*, and I, I can think only of that which shall be, and I tremble. Poetry (real poetry) always seemed to me to be (I thought, tying up my tenth sack) a quest for signs taken up at the heart of a world *that asks only to answer*, questioned, it is true, according to a given inflection of the voice. War, due to that excruciating doubt it instils in us regarding ourselves and the universe, can only paralyse the conversation between the poet and the world, founded on a reciprocal *abandon.* Whether one fights or merely 'stands guard', war is perpetual *presence* to us, and if one attempts to forget about it as I tried just now, having reached the very edge of the poetic exchange, everything suddenly collapses, duplicitously undermined by the presence denied that wreaks its vengeance. The eternal grass is surrendered to the scythe, the eternal foliage to winter, that eternal peasant who is my friend again becomes the soldier on holiday who returned the other day, who still carried on his deep chest the little plaque of polished bone on which can be read:

Dragoon
Fernand Cherpillod
Squadron 4

and, tomorrow perhaps, will depart again.

I swear to you, it is not a matter of mirages; it is the bare and strict truth.

At the very moment when the clear bell of a village outside any hour began to ring, soon followed by other bells all along the valley (we loaded tall carts with the second crop on the hill; the men left well before the end, without looking back), I *saw* the immense landscape up to the mountains change abruptly in appearance, becoming, from one minute to the next, just like an inscrutable face. In vain, in the weeks that followed, did I hope to seek the most concealed fields, at the edge of forests or enclosed by hedges, I had only to bend down to a flower—mute—towards a branch—still—to understand that they too already *knew* and that they could no longer say anything to men.

Until when?

I am myself out of habit, like an empty hotel room that remembers its absent guests, like an abandoned crossroads. It is going to rain.

The wind drags along the cement stoop, with the sound of crumpled newspapers, of fat, dried-out birthwort leaves. Then it throws itself into the curtains billowing like sails and pulls from their folds the sad scent of snuffed-out cigars. Milk steams on the big grey tablecloth, near the grey bread and butter the colour of oranges. A pewter spoon is stuck at an angle in a ribbed glass full of a fruit jelly, murky like a dead wine. The wife has gone back to her kitchen. I remain alone in this room with the November morning beginning, like it without vigour, inexplicably happy.

Bullfinch

The foot is unsure on the morning paths, in the December prairies. A thin freeze has spangled the rutted earth; that sparkling register of yesterday's crossings, carts, horses, labourers, becomes mud again at the first impact. One trips, with arms waving so sharply that they rouse from each tree, from each hedge, a storm of birds, soon calmed. And arisen again all taut from its long night of cold wind and naked sky, the country yields to the impact of the gaze, recovers that peace following fulfilment, that somewhat weary gentleness by which it glides at a slow pace towards rest. From blade to blade of grass, the frost becomes dew again; beyond the bunches of alders and ash trees, a wind out of nowhere plays with the village smoke and, just at the edge of the sky, the mountains traced in snow float on a bank of blue fog so fragile and so sad that the heart dares no longer.

The mill sleeps nearby the open locks. What silence in this place where all through October and November seethes the enormous noise of rushing water, when the wheat threshing machine, from dawn to dusk, voices its complaint! The dead surface of the water conforms without a sound to its rocky bed; its crust of carved-out ice lies upon the sand of the shore: a chaos of pale shards of light beneath the reeds and the boughs. Winter (it is that season's customary game) tries to bury the site in a sly temporal absence and, the better to do so, disconcerts the soul by imitating other seasons. Suddenly in the sun it brings to flower a whole bush of clematis. A hedge of hawthorn appears, the hair of a woman in the light, a horse's blond mane left to the wind . . . One approaches and all is extinguished. The hand brings back the mockery of a vine, a string of seeds: hundreds and hundreds of tufts of grey wool. Ah! it is indeed the winter, and time is not abolished! The shadow of the barn, painted in blue-black on the grassy bank, glides forth and uncovers another shadow the colour of snow: a double, discordant calque of frost and shadow which confesses the sun's frailty. The eye stops there for an instant and questions it, then in one leap rises to the tip of the highest ash tree where burns a tiny pink flame, the body of a bird. In the very time of this gaze, the bird sings, a single note—and the whole winter is in it.

*

I think that the man in the prime of his vigour and his strength, and who feels it enough to doubt not his gaze, his hearing, is, to the letter, blind and deaf. I think that only certain extreme states of the soul and the body: fatigue (at the edge of nothingness), illness, invasion of the heart by a sudden suffering maintained at its paroxysm, can return to a man his true strength of hearing and seeing. No allusion, here, to Plotinus' words: 'Close your eyes, so that the inner eye may open.' It is a question of the supreme instant when communion with the world is given to us, when the universe ceases to be a perfectly legible spectacle, entirely inane, to become an immense spray of *messages*, a concert of cries, songs, gestures ceaselessly beginning again, in which each being, each thing is at once sign and carrier of signs. The supreme instant also at which man feels his laughable inner royalty crumble, and trembles, and gives in to the calls coming from an undeniable *elsewhere*.

Of these messages, poetry alone (is it necessary to say it?) is worthy to suggest some echo. Often it gives up, weeping, for they are almost all muttered on the verge of the ineffable. It awakens from its knowledge, its lips still heavy with absent or mad words that it does not dare repeat—and yet which contain the truth. Or if it dares to repeat them, it does so while seeming to have forgotten their origin, their importance. It divulges in two verses a devastating secret, then falls silent. Eichendorff, in a poem to his dead granddaughter, tells her of the larks that sing above his bleak walk:

I *weep without a word—they bring*
A *message you gave them for me.*

Without his tears, the poet would have heard the song, not the message. It is at the price of all the torment of his grief that he grew to know the terrible secret of the birds. For these two verses contain nothing that resembles a 'poetic image', even a beautiful and touching one. *They speak the strict and entire truth.*

This secret is also yours, bullfinch, little pink flame blown from branch to branch by the wind out of nowhere. And I *knew* it, since that former December, day after day, near the dead water where dead leaves were floating among the foam. 'Ah! that lost voice is not from *here!*' I cried when your first song pierced my heart. One sole note, as if from a somewhat hoarse and yet-so-sweet flute; a lament, a call, a timid prayer . . . 'But *who* laments, then, *who* prays, *who* calls to me beyond this song?' I asked again. And, already, I knew the answer.

But today it is not your message that I can hear, it is your song alone where all of winter triumphs, that song that keeps the very time of winter like a heart without courage. At each beat, the soul also totters. It calls to its defence its dearest images, but poetry is without power over this cry erupting higher than any poetry. Lost bird, must one lose oneself with you, and for ever? Must one mock one last time the agonizing memory trying to dispel the frost and the ice, to resurrect a June sky upon the foliage, a flat lock where three swallows blur their flight paths and reflections, a horse burst from the branches and his wild, naked rider? 'It was your friend at harvest time, and there will be other harvests!' but the name that it tries to repeat to me, already I no longer hear it.

The woodcutter with the chest fractured by one of those long firs that hesitate as they topple, bounding suddenly with an unpredictable outthrust upon one of their murderers, the woodcutter, waking from his first rest in days finally dares to turn his head towards the little window at the back of his room. He sees a bit of hill cleansed by the rain, of a gentle, somewhat yellowish green, and on the grey of the sky a fine spray of boughs from a solitary apple tree. A limp wave of tepid wind rolls along the walls up to his face. He is dreaming. March? April? Tomorrow he will open his eyes with surprise, bathed in a light cold and pale like chalk; his son, all black against the blinding window, his lips on the windowpanes, will cause to perish with his breath alone a whole garden of frost that is ceaselessly reborn. It is sad and cosy in this narrow chamber. A just-extinguished oil lamp stands on the commode, next to a stone marten silently crying towards the door. Close by, an iron platter painted in dark red with a wreath of golden leaves holds an empty glass, a gleaming bottle. A rifle hung on the wall can still be seen, at an angle beneath an old lithography: With the current (a boatman has dropped the oars and sat down next to the young lady passenger whom he amorously embraces; at their feet gives way a mountain of grapes and watermelons upon which they shall soon feast). No one comes, no one calls. The gaunt face, so near, without anguish abandons itself to sleep again.

Narrative

Whoever wants to lose himself, here, must take excessive care. The night itself is peopled with too many lamps to let anyone set off on an adventure; he finds himself back here almost always, alas! and his deviations are so voluntary that he soon gives up, since they are so planned and sort of dictated by a too-obvious 'right track.' But the fatigue of a long walk in the snow, a little forest that I crossed with great effort, my eyes horribly open among hostile presences, felt before they are distinguished, ghosts imperceptibly murmuring their own light, trunks, dried leaves, hollow ice of the ruts and ditches (I groped along through ash, I opened my fingers in a liquid, airy milk), and a whole bewildered territory: ravines, hills, plateaus, strewn with muddled hedges, with reeds and alders in bunches, led me little by little into *strangeness*, that strangeness that is made of the known that one cannot manage to recognize. The man in a city, who has passed from one street to another without knowing it, crossing the maze of stairs, corridors, inner courtyards, offices and workshops that separate them, stands at the threshold of a reopened door, having before him a spectacle, contemplated a hundred times over, of architecture, cars and passers-by—but that he does not recognize. In the space of a second, he is truly *lost*. My whole night was just like that second.

The forest had withdrawn, but the sky, having reappeared, gave me barely a few stars; already the strangeness was beginning, through these new constellations that the gaze composed out of the scattered members of the old ones. There was an instant, made of these bizarre fires, a long, hazy woman who closed her hand like a grape-picker around the cluster of the Pleiades. Then the Pleiades disappeared. A farm rose up in my path. The arch of a barn's bridge straddled the road. I heard, with a little twinge in my heart, the sound of a chain dragged along the pavement, a growl, the abrupt bark of a beast immediately calmed. The steps of a man, more rapid than my own, reached me, surpassed me. The man was whistling a melody that I can still remember and that I hesitate in recognizing; perhaps it was 'Farewell Little Rose':

> *Farewell little rose*
> *white rose of the morning*
> *white rose just opening*
> *in my garden blooming*

Horses and voices could be heard ever closer, three riders passed. The beasts' hooves were sliding around, crushing the soft snow. A lamp shone on a sleeping hedge that the frost had caused to bloom again for a night. The road was more and more populated, the lamps so close together and so bright that I *ought* to have recognized the faces of that inexplicably joyous crowd. 'Faster, Marie! There's another one who'll arrive before us! There won't be any spots left,' said a voice when I passed four elderly ladies in black bonnets, stooped and planting their canes delicately in the snow, far in front of them. Yes, I ought to have recognized that voice, like the air the man drew in, and like this village we've entered, which begins like twenty others with a tall church and ends with an inn, its two 'drinking rooms' and the other room to which the crowd has led me.

*

A room upstairs, the low ceiling made of big jutting beams, the walls painted with a bluish whitewash, so naked, so pure that the gaze struck suddenly and uneasily against trophies (a pink-and- green crest against a branch of cool fir) hanging here and there. A black and polished stove stretched overhead the lightweight arm of its pipe, just like those that were for a long time, with the versets painted on their sides

MY SON GIVE ME YOUR HEART

black on white, the only ornament of reformed churches. The stage (or what I take for the stage) is closed with a flowered cretonne and surrounded on all sides by taut fabrics, dark red and blue-green. Against this ground of indistinct draperies, to the right gleam the instruments of a little orchestra: the dirty white of a keyboard and open sheet music on light lecterns, the silver of clarinet keys, a long flute. Soon, amid the rustling of a room slow to quiet down, a fine and sharp little march rings out. It falls silent. A few hands clap. The stage curtain slides back, hesitating on its rod. Beneath a lamp can be seen a young girl, standing. She must have had a great fright, she must have expected something terrible, for she sought among the faces turned towards her, slowly, someone that she is little by little relieved not to find; the fear and defiance that hardened her face vanish, joy seizes her so abruptly that a shiver of surprise, with murmuring, sweeps the room. She smiles, leans towards the musicians. One of them stands, takes his flute and stops at the foot of the stage. As lost as I felt, so ready for any surprise, ah! never would I have been able to guess (nor anybody among those bodies suddenly tense around me in a vertiginous silence) what happened then and which was, yes, the birth of music, a song not an echo but the very presence of love. Two notes, two words sufficed to compose that charm that none of us could have broken. A song was being born at the same time as love, sung in a slow bass against a naive flute counterpoint. The voice fell silent. The curtain of flowery cloth tried to close again, fell back again. We could see the young girl sitting, her head a bit tilted, lost in her long blue dress (as pale as the blue of the walls), her hands on her knees like two flowers. No one dared to shatter that grace. The young man put his flute to his lips again ... And all of us plunged into the delirium of a dead-end love. From song to song (between them there were only increasingly briefer pauses) the voice arose more desperate and more imperious. The man had climbed on stage, he was obstinately lowering his eyes, a large furrow at his brow like the trace of a soot-stained finger; it is towards him, towards him that the young girl was turning! and all of a sudden her naked arm beat the air slowly like a wing, she laid her hand on his sombre shoulder. Everyone had risen; the last song, savagely punctuated by blasts from the brass (for the whole orchestra was playing now, the clarinet more shrill than a war fife), burst out like a deliverance, the only possible deliverance, that of elopement:

> Between eleven and midnight
>   the dragoon came to take her
> My love hurry and come to me
> I hold my horse by the bridle
> The regiment is set to leave

The man seemed to grow taller with each word. He was trembling. He lowered his flute abruptly, looked at us, his face hardened with a sudden resolution, slowly turned his head ...

'Claire!'—a cry burst out near me that cut short our delirium; a little old man, his head bare, his shoulders stained with snow, was running towards the stage through a crowd of statues. The young girl drew her hand to her bosom, closed her eyes, opened them again, followed the man like a sleepwalker and disappeared.

There came a sort of intermission. To the left of the stage, around a round table loaded with glasses and wine, a waltz was born of a shimmer of trumpets. Little girls stepped among the benches, pulling from little bags some caramels with sayings, lottery tickets rolled in a metal ring:

> Love's unspoken name
> Burns more than a flame

Little by little this supernatural night became dreary like the others again. The celebration resembled every winter celebration in every village. The curtain (that they had managed to close again) opened once more on a 'men's choir.' No one spoke of the strange scene. I left. Two men met me before the door. They were speaking quite loudly and, already far from them, I distinctly heard this shred of a sentence: '... the young lady of the castle. No, no, her father knew nothing.' The place was deserted. I took one of the roads, at random. The lamps grew farther apart; beneath the last one, at the edge of the night, something dark stirred in the snow. I saw entangled bodies, I thought it was a fight, but a pleading voice started again: 'Louis, Louis, let me go! Henri, you have no heart! Oh! my God, you know very well that they went that way! Louis, Louis, leave me! Oh! they are already far away, he's capable of anything. I—'

The voice fell silent, other voices murmured something, in the tone used to calm frantic animals. They saw me approach without surprise. His wrists in the fists of his two kneeling friends, the sprawling man's face was thrown back under the lamp, his lips ragged.

*

You who still believe in miracles, oh! should you want to seek that lost village! Remember: the farm and the arch of its barn's bridge, the hedge beneath the lamp, the tall church. The stair of the inn has a double banister, and beneath the winders are two of those iron fences where the dragoons tie up their horses on Sunday afternoons...

Under three lamps

the dark table where stir eight red hands for an exchange
of coloured maps

the chalk the chalkboard and the sponge the gleaming
crimson of a pipe an empty shot glass on the plate ringed in
gold

an exhausted cigar smokes obliquely towards the light

Pigeons

The two pigeons are right there in the big grey and rose basket. Will they really need to be killed, dear Aimé? I've never received any, how should it be done? It's a new form of death that needs to be invented and who will take this on? The death of chickens, of rabbits, of pigs, that of calves brought in on the carts, tangled in their net like Agamemnon awaiting the axe, and the death of large beasts is known as well. But these beautiful motionless birds beneath this cloth that's being unstitched? They shine like asphalt after the rain, and are iridescent like it, placed on their feet like tripods of pink sugar. They're so calm that they barely seem birds. It's that they aren't yet, I mean they don't know how to fly. You took them off the high iron beam that holds up the bridge of your barn. They stay up there all day, letting out shrill little cries when their parents feed them from their beaks. One morning one of them dropped to the pavement; its wings betrayed it. That's the moment to take them, before flight has hardened their flesh, and you gave them to me. A little boy has left his village, across the fields, his two arms held out to the right, pressing against his hip the basket in which he would disappear completely—and this basket you give me, too. It is grey and rose, made from two types of wicker, the one bare, the other with its bark. It is beautiful and heavy, it is like those you see in October orchards when the branches are suddenly stirring (although the air is still): a foot appears, probing the void, in search of the next step. The man slowly tilts the bag that girds him like a harness; the apples roll into the basket one by one.

All this, I ought to have gone up to you and told it to you. The road is not so long that separates us. And yet it's not idleness that holds me back, but fear. Forgive me. Fear of a whole dead universe that stands between you and me and that would have to be rolled aside like a corpse. A dead road under a dead sky. A black country, a white country, still stiff yesterday and softening already today, disjointed, broken, where the mist, as if the abyss were taking them back, removes entire hills. It would demand being strong as a tree; eyes closed upon its strength, fists tightened, to place a foot upon this treacherous shoreline, and to cross in one leap, like quicksand, this place where being and non-being merge. Oh! few things, it's true, would suffice to restore courage: at the edge of the road, the lungwort plant, coarse to the touch like union fabric. A green stain of wheat, victorious wheat from the snow, or even a single mouthful of less bitter air ... Aimé, I wait as well for the inner shock that lifts you like wine, this certainty of a miraculous unforeseeable Future ...

I will not witness these works of winter so pretty to see done in their monotony that befits a pastime. When there is no wood left to saw or split, when the snow prevents long pauses at the edge of the trimmed hedges where the fascines are bundled, it is time to prepare the bindings for the bundles (for those who still make them) with the long rye hay beaten by the flail. Near a narrow stable window, half your body tightly encircled by the light, the other mingled with shade where the straw gleams softly, undone and twisted like hair, you're sitting, your fists closed around the coarse plait that's twisted and pulled. If the sun by the green windowpane comes to touch this wheat and give back its tawny August colour, here is reborn in the blackness a whole afternoon harvest, in its odour of sweat and hot hay, your bare shoulder, your broad, bare chest breaking through the sky like a swimmer out of calm waters, the glazed pitcher dripping with light and water that falls from the sky to your lips. Are they reborn for you as well, these images of a long searing fatigue? Do they make the day's half-rest appear deeper and vaster to you? But you are their master; they vanish when you wish, when they should, whereas me they assail—and like a reaper, with a foot on their nest, trapped in a swarm of fierce wasps, I can no longer resist them.

I should take a chance by means of the *object*, like when you twist bindings or weave baskets. But no one harvests here any longer; the barn is empty and the baskets unused, for the orchards no longer have fruit. Fortunate man! Beyond the little window you see a January garden with two sleeping hives, and you think: 'Let the sun appear, and the bees come out.' You say again to yourself: 'If the snow doesn't come tomorrow, I will go gather the cut alders.' The children's clogs can be heard against the pavement, school is over. The pigeons leave the fountains and settle among the rocks at the doorstep, because they know it's time for their grain. They wait. Mine are always there, side by side, pressed against the bare wicker. I caress the soft slate of the feathers. You could say that they're waiting too—but for *what*?

Behind the dead leaves on the branches of beech trees and the dried meadowsweet stalks, the vast stretch of prairies beneath the sky where the milk-white clouds descend. Three scarlet facades still alive; here and there, groups of weightless trees of a green-grey. Snow slowly disappears, allowing to be reborn the beautiful green of the wheat, the fields of wool.

Fernand and his footman strip a fallen oak tree with an axe. In Aimé's barn, the long monotonous ringing of the flails.

Farewell to a Dead Road

For Edmund Thevoz

Thevoz, you too know it well: this procession of solemn poplars, this double row of living columns, vertiginous, that guided the traveller towards your town and your house, they were thrown down, they carved them up with saws, axes and the wedges of metal driven with a sledge hammer right into their flesh. There is nothing left, between the grassy banks, but an unwelcoming road, pale and hardened beneath too much sun like a river seized by ice—a dead path.

Will we be able to save our memories?

I long believed in the omnipotence of this oblique memory by which our interior night, deaf and closed to our calls, suddenly lights up *and calls to us*, when the golden slant of the magical ray illuminates in the darkness the shimmering heap of buried minutes, or sometimes the lone flame of an instant from most distant childhood. (And even if all this shadow persists in remaining shadow, a blind scent, a voice without voice rekindles and rises up to us.) All that Time gave us and could not, I thought, take back from us. Our sole treasures.

Will they be little by little taken from us? This too, like all the rest?

Yet a man's memory is something *unique*! This thing that is mine alone, that assures me of my most profound identity! The pure salt slowly deposited by temporal swells . . . To whom do we have recourse, if it begins to lose its flavour?

I'm scared, Thevoz. These axes between Missy and Saint-Aubin that toppled the high murmuring wall, I feel them inside me dully continuing their despoiling. The wound there healed over (barely here and there in vague scars of grass) is in me, it begins to open up. This road forever sleeping in me is no longer safe. It strips itself bare like the other. The trunks totter, wounded in turn. No longer are these the winds of the past that innocently rocked the treetops against the brown and rosy clouds of summer. The ceaseless quivering of the leaves becomes fever and the mortal shivering of things condemned. Time will take back these gifts.

*

Ah! Why have I come back down, league upon league, along a dark Broye in late autumn until I reached this mutilated road! But how can one stop the obsessive pursuit of a call? Every day I felt it overtake me, imperious and vague all at once, become little by little a species of sorrowful supplication ceaselessly penetrated by the threat or presence of death. These trees at the instant of death, did they perhaps remember the adolescent who had loved them and caressed them long ago before settling back for an hour of shade at their fraternal trunks? This *impassive theatre* has always made me smile: no, Nature feels our adorations, she calls, she too desires exchange; still more, she lives on it. These trees recalled our friendship; they recalled my step near to them in the summer night when out from the low inn, far from my glass still alone amid the smoke, I looked up to see sparkling and escaping up there, between the banks of dark foliage, a thin stream of stars. They were going to die and they were calling out to me.

Without my knowledge, other tiny deaths (but is there a hierarchy to death?) were preparing me for the spectacle of their massacre. The night before leaving, in the field where three great bluish fires were smoking, that frantic mouse that leaps suddenly out of the furrow and that one of us knocks cold with the whip handle. It was still struggling, flipped over on its back, its back legs going limp, rigid, limp . . . And on the road, at the first step, the still-warm body of the weasel, its muzzle resting in a puddle of blood the colour of carnations.

The valley where I advanced among the invisible shoulder-blows of the wind lay also half-dead beneath the closed sky, verdigris, violet, with the pale marks of the tombs from village to village, as souring to the eye as to the throat a wine that turns, a sloe picked from the hedges before the frost. Between two gusts, at the corner of the stubble, I tried to bite into my icy bread, then started back on the road in haste, greeting from time to time some gatherers of grain, standing, shivering, their blue hands in the pretty rose of the tobacco plants. Unending march towards *je ne sais quoi* waits for me there and calls me, so slow to leave the horizon! Day recedes again, But I no longer need its light. Corcelles, Dompiere, Domdidier . . . The road swerves abruptly towards the other side of the plain. It becomes more sombre with every step. No matter, I could follow it without opening my eyes, blind it with a hundred bursting suns from my memory! It touches against a low thicket, overtakes a strip of still water, runs along mass graves of beetroots and cabbage. A swarm of moribund leaves. A swarm of starlings. The first farm on my right. The first hedge of dahlias. Saint-Aubin appears, its pointed church, enclosed by two flaming cherry trees.

Saint-Aubin, the church always above the little forest of gravestones, the bishop in his mitre, yellow and violet, standing on the eight-sided stone basin, the bitter chrysanthemums that ripen everywhere for the dead . . . But today all these recovered things cannot grant me any ease. Will *they* give it back to me one more time, those who were waiting for me at the edge of the path, ready to pass their shadow arms over my shoulder, feigning in all their foliage a fresh rain suspended over my slumber! I turn my head: the road is empty. I responded too late to their call. The road is a corpse lying in its pit of grasses under the gloomy face of bare sky.

*

Thevoz, you now live in a tower rising tall over the city which assails you night and day with cries, odours and fumes. And me, I live still in this Jorat where the spring is so long to arrive. It is a March Sunday. There is a bit of snow in the garden. The cats attempt a first nap at the edge of the flowerbeds. I think of you. I write. We are both quite far from the town where you were born, from your house, from your garden (in the summer, a tamarix leaning against the road a little green-and-rose cloud). Far from this road I love so dearly, and I know you loved too. We must say goodbye to it as if to a dead woman, since we will never pass by here again. Never again . . . Yet is there not in the deepest depths of our heart, like a stubborn and timid spring outside even the ruins of memory, this voice barely a breath that announces to us the end of Time and that all the beloved things erased for an instant by illusory death, *our* eyes finally opened again will see them reborn one by one in their all-presence, when the Day has come—when there will be no more days?

To say the works of the men in this colourless countryside under a soft sky amused by tufted clouds. Aimé sews the trefoil in small, precise, staccato gestures. The loggers fill the ravine with smoke. An old man sets ablaze light piles of dried leaves.

The March Woodcutter

Long ago I held the belief for many years that winter, in separating him from the world, restores him to himself. *Winter,* I wrote, *as it cuts out our corporeal silhouette with sharp shears against the snow, preserves for our minds its finest, its most lucid ridges.* This came, I must say, from reflecting upon Mallarmé's verse:

> *Winter, season of serene art, winter lucid*

and this vision of the diamond-spirit, brother of ice and hoarfrost, and by them purified, it was also, without a single doubt, Mallarmé's vision that unconsciously I made my own ... Today I believe there are two kinds of men: those who *die upon the seasons* (to adopt the cryptic utterance of Rimbaud), and those who go along neither noting them nor living them. And for that first kind of man, winter is truly a death. Yes, the diamond-spirit can deceive itself and wrest from its icy enchantment the certitude of its own existence. But what does the heart become? It cannot feed upon itself, since it does not live but through exchange and it has been refused any exchange. It stops, or, if it still beats, it is with a beating so weak that it becomes an affliction. The heart has no understanding of that *repose of nature* that the blind report; its rest is pain. And this repose of nature too is not rest, it is pain. Who hasn't sensed it, for example, while walking through the winter forest? The blind have spoken of its 'winter slumber', they've taken the vast rolling mountaintops they thought were asleep for the giant body of some princess in the grip of a magical languor, dreamlessly awaiting her Awakener, whereas now there is no more forest but one, but ten, but a hundred, but thousands of trees each of which is *alone* among its brothers, and suffers. Halt: this muffled silence of the snow, does it not burst out like a cry of suffering? The heart hears it (even if the spirit amuses itself with the play of shadows and crystals); it recognizes its brother in each of these rooted beings around him, these grand vegetal heights bowed beneath the burden of their hoarfrost, fatally stiffened, and displaying here and there a scrap of rose and orange flesh in the wound of a broken branch. A tiny little chickadee (a crested tit, I believe) flies from one low branch to another, tiny as its cry, that cry more fleeting than a glimmer of hoarfrost, this cry that is a kind of lament, of desolate call, where our heart and the forest recognize their own lament and their own call.

Heart deprived of exchange, heart edging into agony . . . The diamond-spirit may contemplate living under the dead sparkling of its facets, the heart is no longer but an indefinite waiting, the heart makes its food of the slightest *sign*: a patch of grass sprung from the edge of the snow, the earth beneath the rotting leaves pierced through by a tuft of tender stems . . . A miserable quest, like that of the hungry street peddler in the paths of autumn's last days, when he drops his too-heavy bags and feels around through the grass and the fog for the apples pierced by the ravens! A relentless quest, incessantly taken up again from sign to sign, from collapse to collapse until that evermore beautiful hour when the heart, at the brink of despair, suddenly senses that the world has been restored to it.

'Suddenly' is at once right and wrong here, for one certainly senses that *something* has changed abruptly (and it's the light), but it is only little by little that *all things* appear to us to transform, little by little that the reconciliation is consummated. We walk in a new light, and we see that this winter road, where for so long the hollowed ice of the puddles burst beneath our step, is no longer a winter road: on the riverbanks, niveoles will begin to bloom (these are false snowdrops less delicate than the true ones). The new road climbs up into the new light. Louis plants a new walnut tree. —*You are sweet to think of the passers-by still to come.* —*Oh! Well, there we are, I had foremost in mind those who will take their 'ten o'clock'.* Who, even yesterday, would have *dared* to consider the 'ten o'clock' of hay-baling time? Today, Louis's sentence has not yet concluded when we see, in the shadow that frosts their hard, golden shoulders with blue, the hay workers seated with laughter by the bread and wine, and the sun-bitten horses rummaging with their noses through a heap of wilted grass . . . —*There you have it, I'm too late in getting to it*, Louis says, *look, he weeps already like the vine*. He's right. I caress the young bark, I watch its sap pour down, as beautiful as our blood. But the path heads off again. The tree and the man over there are no longer anything more than two friends stopped at the side of the road, time enough for brief greeting. I advance into the heart of a pale and sullen country trembling, like a naked butterfly, at the threshold of its birth. Another friend welcomes me, and the hand I take in mine is a new hand, smooth and golden and no longer the aching winter hand bitten by ice and frost.

March woodcutter! Blue woodcutter with tawny hands, face newly kissed touched by the sun, turning to me this long blue gaze in which a new flame burns, that laugh I had once thought dead, it was time, was it not? We had reached the end of our strength. It all begins again. The thin crimson wicker you spin between your fingers seems to come alive. And the gesture you make suddenly with your body, like a miller boy who, the sack of wheat fallen from his shoulder, stands straight up with a deep sigh, what does he want to say except that the awful burden slips at last from our hearts, from our shoulders, that finally we are *delivered*!

Our long walk through a rainy country brought us to these few minutes at the edge of a silver lake, pale and polished. We cease to speak. The silence was so heavy, so calm; the moment more delicate than the countryside far off behind us, slowly reclaimed by a translucent fog.

Gustave Roud

Air of Solitude

For Maurice Chappaz

. . . But I want to tell you about another unknown country. From Lens, from Randogne, we are crossing the mountains that overlook these towns, then a small valley, then a chain of hills that look like sailboats, until we reach the shoreline of a great glacier, a surface unbroken and flat, all settled among round-peaked mountains, marked here and there with rocks, whose opaque, snowy field gives the impression of fleeing on sight. The eyes desiring the infinite well up when they see! Also, nothing changes, not in the rarefied air, nor in the unmoving masses, nor in the dull white of the expanse. This is a desolate land akin to the setting of the Dead Sea, whose name it nearly takes as its own, being known as the Dead Plain. Passing through, we were like sailors, and thus did we contemplate the sky where a squall seemed bound to come down upon our heads, a beautiful violet opening. Yet still, eager and full of appetite as I was before space . . .

In a low voice, one more time, I read over this page from one of your letters, my dear friend. Marked here and there with sombre lines, the lifeless white of my hands in the miserly light of late winter, it seems itself to come from these lost and lofty regions you have loved. *Loved*, no one could draw the wrong conclusion; your tone is not that of a curious traveller with an eye out for just any spectacle, but indeed of a man who has made a true encounter, that is to say, an exchange. This Dead Plain lives in you. But that your lines should so powerfully invoke it; this is not all that has made me reread them. There's something else in them than just the presence of the poet, something at the limit of the unformulated, that only two or three words suggest and that nonetheless bursts forth upon the mind, indisputable: a fated solitude.

*

Perhaps, at the same time that I'm speaking with you from such a distance, you have gone back up to those blankets of desolate snow? Perhaps you were able (what the downpour that had arisen had kept you from doing with your men) to build an igloo, climb back down, bitterly surrounded by the naked elements: air, ice and rock, to the profound human bareness and appease— for how many hours?—this incurable appetite for space. You are standing (perhaps) on the bow of a black rock, above an inexorably frozen sea; you do not come to space, but it comes to you. The mouthful of air at your lips sharp as the frost, it knew not of other lips and the wind full of pity brings it to you from *elsewhere*. Am I mistaken, dear friend? Have you not arrived at the moment of yourself when the poet, victim of his difference, tears himself in a blind, violent start from the universe imprisoning him, and perseveres, at the price of a ferocious austerity, to fall upon his *true* face at last? This appetite for space, this march, always taken up again, towards elsewhere, it's an obscure desire that guides them now. Ah! to find at last the lost region, barren, inviolate, the bare site that might welcome the bareness of my heart and mind, the dead and faithful mirror in which I appear to me. You've found your Dead Plain, you will discover still more places seized by a deeper silence, where, in an air still rarer, will triumph only the beat of your heart and brain (the structure of the mind is *metric*, said a delirious Hölderlin); where will be given to you, yes, the mirage of a solitary knowledge . . . But the time will come, sailor of the ice, to come back down to another, more painful knowledge. The absolute of solitude lies not in those high deserted places—it lies among men.

*

Among men . . . And yet those surrounding me today in sweeping lands of pale soft colours, alone, or the reins in their grip near a cart, or a ploughshare, their lives are open like a flower; one by one I pluck them with the heart or the gaze. It feels good to lean against this toppled oak, bark barely cooled, where I set down your folded pages and, on top of them, my extinguished pipe, for a small, indecisive wind was struggling to take flight, hot, cold, hot, cold—one wing in spring, one wing in winter. The two seasons lie intertwined like a pair of wrestlers, and the combat's the same, pinnings, pauses, furtive rests, sudden moments of peace, up to my feet where bloom inside a nest of dead leaves and oakum, red or blue, like Easter eggs, the lungworts and the squills. There is also, Chappaz, near a dirty snowbank, a lone windflower peeking out, as pure as a star. I would have liked to paint you the slow victory of early spring here. I dream of an unsurprising voice, tender and monotonous, that would resemble it. It begins with the dragoons on Sunday roads. —*Are you saddling up this afternoon? —Why not?* A gay clapping of hoofs in the mud which mingles against the facades and quiets beneath the creaking gold lion. Then, at morning's end, the sower of oats freezes upon the hill, his heart seized: the larks . . . Ah! the torment of the poet without a voice, all his woeful silence taking him by the throat when this tawny and fletched arrow springs out from the rough grass and becomes song! He pauses in thought, one hand upon the hard shoulder of his friend; I too was born for this joy, to be nothing but this drunken jubilation, headstrong, suspended from delirium to ecstasy, always nearer the light, always closer, light at last . . . *Nostra sirocchia allodola*, these alone among the poets. are your brothers, saints as well. The whole Spiritual Canticle is to be sung as high as the heavens to the heights of heaven, its fluttering of feathers soaked up like a mist by the inner light:

A las aves ligeras
leones ciervos gamos saltadores
montes valles riberas
agua aires ardores . . .

*

They quiet down now, one by one. In the mirror of the lock, the sun slips towards its reflection. The rooftops are stained with smoke. My friend the dragoon there upon his horse leaves behind the young wheat flattened out by the iron roller like a holiday tablecloth. A wood-cutter climbs back up the ravine, crosses the bridges of vines, sickle in his fist, the other grasping a rose bundle of spurge laurel. One, two, three still ploughs . . .

It is the time when the lives of men upon themselves bend back. We believed they were rooted in our own hearts; we sense, while they are departing towards their true home, the great absence reclaiming its authority over this slowly deserted heart. Absolute of solitude . . . Nothing hinders its triumph, I say to you, Chappaz. Laughter, words, hands shaken, long labours side by side, the silence always returns, more merciless than that up on the Dead Plain. The silence of men and the silence of things: the river has grown silent, the wind has grown silent. The poor anemone at my feet, the last being to offer me the alms of its gaze, he also closed up like a star extinguished on the threshold of the shadow.

It is not yet the sun of the 'hot evenings' that tan the reapers and the foliage, when out from beneath the already dark orchards suddenly shines some copper shoulder or face. Behind a weak vapour the colour of ash, the sun releases rays without vigour to beat upon the breeze their feeble and clumsy wings, like those of a bat. All turns to ash in this ashen sun, the entire world loses its substance and its weight, becomes brittle under one's gaze. We walk upon a green ash that is the grass, without a single flower. How many days, how many suns upon the bare branches, before the flower and the fruit? We still drag behind us, caught within our flesh and our gazes, all the waiting and horror of winter. But near at hand, the first swipe of the scythe, this clean and rapid gliding, as it slices the tender stalks, slices all that ties us to the dead season, and sets us free. The break consummated at last, the promise kept once again, the rediscovered certainty of an intoxicating possession. Calm rustling heard rising up in the heart of the new grass, like a fount long dry, like a heart beginning to beat again! The reaper swings his two arms the rosy red of a doll. To the teeth of the rake that his little child lifts and dips in the last ray, still clings, floats and comes loose at a mysterious signal, a long winter spiderweb.

Point of View

In order to traverse so many years again, sometimes going back down a hill is all it takes: as soon as you reach the river, your adult footprint has disappeared; an adolescent foot breaks the dried reeds, crumples poetry, the dead leaves, and redraws in the sand of the bank the same imprint that long ago was wiped clean by the great waters. Less a few tears, the sharper sense of unlimited ignorance, the disturbances of the blood tamed or transfigured into continuous power—all this is but nuance and does not introduce any profound difference between the ancient reverie and the new, along the same depthless waters beneath its shell of glimmering reflections. What does this world *want to say*? And if it has no response to offer us, why does it relentlessly feign discourse? Now as in past days, the simultaneous presence and flight of the waters at my feet perpetually murmur *something* undefinable and I give a start when the blackbird chants (night is coming) an undeniable question.

The old excuse of these idle hands, the day when on a sign from the heavens all the men outside their too-warm homes were populating the fields with horses, carts, glistening shovels, it was truly a kind of call that came to me from everywhere, while to other men an order was given. The world said to them: Go. It said to me: *Will you not come?* And I entered with the last sun beneath the low branches, like today. An old willow with its heart full of soil looks like a hanging garden, so much does it feed the plants and shrubs woven into its own wreath. The path emerges suddenly among the dead reeds, and the thicket begins. There are always, like slabs of yellow rock, the close-cut trunks where one sits, hands dragging through the leaves. I am waiting, how many years now I have waited—and what answer? Out of the dried leaves, golden, blue, grey as bread, slate, or canvas, emerge the spindles of new plants. Two stems of spurge laurel sway their rosy wax blossoms, and one's nostril, nearly right away, bathes in the sickening sweet smell. Here and there, large circles of scattered feathers; each marking the murder of a bird, but the birds sing as they have never sung. There is that which is dead and finishes rotting, and there is that which is born and mixes inextricably into it and timidly pushes it aside or feeds off of it. The soul and the body both hesitate also at the threshold of the new life. This hesitation, will it once again prove fatal for them, and the fruitless vigil be prolonged? Where will they find the supreme courage to lose themselves, to surrender? Perhaps this is what the world was expecting from them, and its call sought neither master nor witness but accomplice. The accomplice who for years refuses, for fear of betraying his most essential being. Look at this man, says the river, who knows not how to leave behind his human pride and join us, and who wishes to understand before he should feel! Let him make a river of himself, and no longer will he try in vain to spell out my language.—Let him become a tree, says the tree, and he will know what the wind and earth say, and the weight of this hot golden gown that the sun gives us and takes from us at the threshold of night! Man, the river responds, laughable, silent man whose hands lie among the leaves and sand, consider your brother the woodcutter who walks along me, looking innocent; I hate him, I know what he is contemplating, but you may take him as an example, for at the sight of the trout he is about to catch, he makes a fish of himself. Remember it: you will not understand a thing that you have not deeply resembled.

Will I obey?

Beautiful sun, dying sun that touches my hands one last time, one and then the other, one the colour of blood, the other of a pale rose, you colour also the hill beyond the trunks like a heavy fabric of branches over which the fringe of the icy shadow extends second by second. Let me wrest myself away from this deceitful council murmured incessantly around me, let me follow you step by step up to the summit where your daily death takes place! I walk along a stream of black oil between the tufts of closed anemones and the primroses.

The ash trees catch fire and die out one by one, the raven before me flies from a shaded branch to a fiery branch. Sun! Sole true presence, you who from morning on places upon my shoulder the fraternal hand of an eternal travelling companion—and when I look down at the dust that your radiance glorifies I sense obscurely the Other Presence that your presence *signifies*, sun, ah! how I would lose my life to imitate other lives, to bury myself halfway under earth like the weighty tree, to sprawl upon sand and rock like the weighty river, to drag my feet throughout my labour like those around me who *accept*, until the Angel of Death turns their faces against the furrow they had begun! *Will you not come with me?* The reaper asks me submerged up to the chest in the enigma of flowers in the folly of flowering, and a look so pure rises up within his innocent eyes that tremblingly I divert my own. *Will you not become one of us?* say men who come and go, who laugh, talk, count, beautiful as animals or machines. Sun, sun, is it still a creature who speaks to you, one that a ray conjures up, that a finger of shadow destroys, that the wind blows away like a husk upon the world? 'You made your conscience the centre of the world and of yourself,' a voice whispers to me, 'and for this reason both you and the world have been devoured. What are you still waiting for? There is no spring for those who have not dared to die.'

The enigma emerging at the birth of each spring—and the anguish, the fear of leaving it behind with no reply! The winter, using with regard to the mind a kind of complicity, reduces the world nearly to a collection of signs as conventional and rigid as writing; the window can be shut upon a snow-swept landscape as one might close a book. Texts disappear; we recover our freedom. Nothing more impossible than an exchange, if we cross our threshold. Each light, each star shines its strict shine; churches enumerate the hours; the snow keeps count of our steps. Our breath itself, by which we should be tied to the universe, it is a small vapour rounded and precise, rolling distinctly towards the moon.

But now that the presence of the world is unavoidable, and enclosed within it night and day—our sleep shredded by its birds, struck by the surge of the new wind within the foliage, and its gaze clearly gorged on harmonies from birth—the old desire once again seizes us to resolve this glistening enigma. In former times, it demanded a leap of fifteen leagues across the prairies, the villages, the cool forests; sleep beneath an ash tree would send you on your way at the break of day in the dew and glimmering dreams: the enigma was suppressed by a sort of unprecedented adherence.

But we cannot always surrender ourselves: for as intoxicating as it may become, the confusion of he who questions with he who is questioned is no more than sporadic. Tonight, it is to a horrifically distinct being that a frail, blossoming cherry tree (the last to bloom, its tiny white hand tremoring imperceptibly) poses anew the mysterious question.

And there will never be a response.

Angel

There are things that ought to excite to the utmost degree the curiosity of men, says Baudelaire, and which, judging by their ordinary lifestyle, inspires no curiosity. Where are our dead friends? Why are we here?—he continues, raising further questions. How to answer? How to answer, if not to say that none of our friends are dead, and that it's up to us to not be *here*? Or, better perhaps, letting Alain-Fournier have his say: *When I will have enough images, that is to say, when I have the leisure and the strength to no longer gaze at any but those images in which I see and feel the world living and dead mingled with the ardour of my heart, then, perhaps, I will succeed in expressing the inexpressible. And this shall be my poetry of the world.*

You laugh at these solemn quotations, and I can already hear your reproach: a June evening is not spent with questions on one's lips (especially questions posed by another) but with a sainfoin stem, a sage leaf, a daisy. Yes, and at once, without even a thought, they are thrown away. As for the questioning, it takes root in the furthest depths of one's being; it is reborn with the

66

breath, with each beat of the heart. Where are our dead friends? Why are we here? But what is *here*? And is it not a little our fault if we do not make of it a perpetual *elsewhere*? It is not a matter of escaping by way of reverie or poison, nor of any absence of body or soul. Simply of an insufficient presence. There is a certain poverty, an avarice of our heart, of our gaze, of our spirit, that makes *here* always identical to itself, conferring on it all the inexorability of a prison. Indeed, that certain obsession with Heaven, is it not born of a secret inability to *see* this world at hand, whereas if we knew how to see it, for us it would become Heaven?

I am not playing with words.

At the very instant the rain stops, a warbler's song begins, liquid and pure like the rain, droplet by droplet into the heart of the leaves. The prairies' fleece, out to the horizon, glimmers and steams beneath a ray of white sun. Praise for water, praise for light: not a flower keeps its silence. And what is asked of us if not to *participate*, in stillness, head raised and lips closed? Abandon, gift, this alone. And the scythe is not far away, these flowers know it. But for man alone the Angel of Death is this black sparrowhawk turning in the dusk above the villages, searching among the clumps of trees for the roof that bears the sign, the crimson stain of tiles to plummet towards, like a stone, wings clipped, without the quiver of a feather.

A sail tilts, the cold wind hollowing it out like a winnowing basket. All the village girls in a boat overloaded with bodies and laughter, marked with a single blue boy, oars dead.

Pigeon

To Hans Grossrieder

More beautiful than the crosses which have lost their lustre on the other inns, their lions eroded by rust, this painted pigeon, this pure pigeon above the threshold, wings closed! Pigeon of welcome and farewell, squeaking more than a rock dove just barely, snared within the sky and the season, snared within their life, snow in the snow, cloud among the summer clouds, a blue wing a golden wing when the sun descends to the hills, limestone pigeon like the June road, iron pigeon sweeter to the eyes than the feathered dove, hollow pigeon pecking at star-wheat, perched forever on the verge of flight, I greet you, and your shadow without weight your beak on my hand close to the glass of hard wine . . .

But to this silent greeting the suspended creature makes no response. She who ripens peacefully with the sun, rose and golden, a shiver crosses over her, her breast goes out and darkens to slate. The snout of a sudden cold wind rummages in the tufts of linden. And, timidly, drop by drop on the cobblestones, the shingles, on the fresh hay and the foliage, the June rain falls like a universal whisper, a presence multiplied to infinity . . . No, Rose. From the doorway you gesture to me, but I will not enter the dark empty room. Leave me be in this downpour sweeter than sleep and that comes down in thousands of delicate fingers to bring forth the deep memories! Little maid in this gown of pink and blue bouquets prettier for being so clumsily worn, you haven't dared to put back on the coral necklace that made the dragoons laugh that Sunday. It was your first Sunday, one could well see, you didn't know how to respond to them, you laughed too much, you laughed poorly, you poured clumsily the large litres of light wine, and Maurice's rudeness brought you to tears. You sat down (that's not allowed) at the empty table, near me; I saw one of your weary hands trembling at your knees and the other sliding two fingers under the red necklace that was suddenly too tight around your throat. It is raining, little maid, it is raining to the depths of the sky, to the depths of the countryside of leaves and the fields of beleaguered blooms. And behind the rain, at the ends of the earth, sings the cuckoo. You smile a little, you feel the thin coins of your tip money against your fingertips. And I, I listen through the long fluttering of the downpour to the two hollow notes descending, awakening in this somnolent heart the miracle of a lost young heart. Nothing is lost, little maid, there is no forgetting for that deep memory in our most secret place like a heavy rose closed up again: made petal by petal of all our lives (and *our* life is only its thin outer petal) year against year, century around century to the void-centre of the birth of time! If we knew what to make of this slumber to which each night returns us, these few hours in which hours by the millions reappear, in which the lone nude man at the fold of his warm sheets is Legion, in which the rose in us reopens and falters, struck in the heart by the arrow of so many calls, if we knew, frightfully undone, opening wide to our eternal root, *who* within us then will answer them!

The cuckoo sings in the rain. Another afternoon rises slowly within me, hill by hill; the road of days past (this empty and pockmarked road that you watch over from your doorway) reappears amid the fresh blue and black grass and the fields of gold that blaze dully under the sun. Near me, three dragoons clink together and set down their gleaming glasses. I watch the three horses in the young imperfect shade of the linden tree, the young men talking and laughing, the laughter suddenly like a flower at their lips. Ah! the bitter mouthful, the bottomless wine of solitude! Adolescence with emptied hands and that no longer even dares reach out, retracted —and all speech impossible—into its inexorable difference! You were alone, little coral-necklaced maid, and the boys laughed at your brusque hands; I was alone as well, but who would have been able to laugh at me, when no one *saw* me? The dragoons left without out a glance at my table; after so many years, I still hear beneath today's sweet rain the steps of their horses growing distant and trampling my heart.

This first privation was necessary, this rupture, this black malaise where the birth of a witness goes on and on, even an unworthy one. The places that see it happen become the witness' mysterious accomplices. I loved this always-empty inn, not a captive of other facades nor standing on the edge of a plaza between the fountain and the plane trees, but solitary, opening into an expanse of sky and prairies, only one village at the lower branch of the linden suspended in evening like a fraternal lamp. It took losing speech to discover the true language of all things; through the innocence offered by the beast and the flower attaining little by little the hidden innocence of men like a harrowing certainty. Long silent discussions, the head bent to the June banks among the abundance of daisies and bees, the swallow's breathless stories and that first night when under a roof of leaves I touched Aimé's horse! Becoming a man again, feeling this heart, for too long closed upon its own blood opening, the hot blood rushed towards living hands! The high shadowy beast against my fingers breathes softly, my empty glass was gleaming among other glasses, ah! little maid, someone there beyond calls me by my name at last . . .

Someone was calling me, I found voice again to respond. You will see, we are not *always* alone. Look at this field nearby where the flowers suffocate under the rain. It's there, just after the hay-gathering, that the dragoons will hold their feast. There they will raise the walls of painted wood, the plaster beams, the hedges without roots, these teetering doors that fall instead of open, all this flimsy scenery that horses surpass in pure long bounds, tearing from the grass a doubled shadow like a mad dead leaf. You will listen, dwarfed at the foot of the facade clacking with flags, to the music swept away by the wind, the cries, the clapping hands, the rumour and silence of a celebrating crowd. In the evening, they will return to you, these simple-hearted boys that frightened you, they will have ribboned shoulders, they will hold by her hand their silken, bare-haired fiancée, and Maurice who has no fiancée will without a word hand to you the necklace of his dead little sister, a sweet necklace, blue as the pigeon on high falling asleep beneath the young moon, a star-grain at his parted beak.

The joy of a moment when I sit down upon the mower, the great closed farm before me, quite near to the fountain, the raucous tireless pigeons . . . how beautiful these houses are, for an hour abandoned! In the morning sun, as if it were Sunday, along the wall of pure snow, the resplendent flowers blossom among the festoons of dark bare vines. The garden washed of its burning by the night showers is a lake of red and yellow flames pierced by hard shadows.

Aimé drives back a large hay cart, unhitches the horses. They have traded kicks, and the youngest mare is bleeding. Aimé, his head bare, his hair black and silver, his gaze of a sometimes muted, sometimes transparent blue, washes the wound with a cloth moistened with water. The sensitive beast jumps and buckles suddenly at the knees, a small boy with his fist at the bridle.

Fernand against the Sky

I will go now among the evening harvests from which
the sun has departed and which sweetly radiate their
golds from beneath the growing shadow. A storm at the
northern horizon buckles in the blue and lead of the
downpour, but at sunrise the clouds linger like solemn
angels, like statues of air and snow, exchanging forms
at their leisure. Mysterious world created, destroyed
ceaselessly with a thousand hands of invisible wind, suspended tonight in its magnificence and majesty. I question it according to the ancient method of the peasants,
lifting my head up to its immense battlefield where the
dying light fights in vain against the vapour and ash,
where islands of soot and silver softly collide and com-
mingle their shorelines. So far from men! So close to
men! Two blue boys build up with stabs of the pitchfork
a cart of sheaves that will soon reach it, and there on top
of the hill is Fernand, standing against the sky, caught
in the sky. Head pressed into the clouds, he turns
towards me his bright eyes where the sudden blaze of
the sunset sharpens a fleeting flame, that blue gaze

without abandon, so calm, where the adolescent gives way to the man, where all the certainty of existence can be read. He picks from the beautiful wall of wheat a single ear that he crushes in his powerful hands, combining them and hollowing them out like a winnowing-fan, blows out the chaff, brings to his lips, one by one, the grains of wheat hard beneath the teeth like a warm crust of bread. The great bare body turns dark once again. A faint gleam still glimmers in the fullness of the powerful shoulder. Fernand against the sky, showing me without a word the first star, trembling between two clouds— and he *touches* it.

How can one depict it in stillness while it knows no rest throughout the day, finding its sole repose in the nocturnal bed-chamber where it bathes in a lake of sleep and shadow—but sleep so light, shadow so fragile that it stirs an icy gust of wind before the dawn, at the first pallor of the horizon, and wrests the human body, little by little, out from its numbness? It is made to touch, to embrace powerfully the lively and inert— that which surrenders and that which resists; it hardly caresses or brushes past, it takes hold. Better still than the gaze, that perpetual fly, that bee without honey, it ties together the world and mankind. He tests, he feels the differences in material, in weight, in heat, by which things separate themselves from him. And by these things that impact him, he gains consciousness of himself and his power. A strong hand no later than dawn pressed against the warm fur of the beasts, wrapped around the scythe handle, dripping with the basin water, kept warm by a ceramic mug of steaming coffee, intertwined with the leather reins wet with dew, lifting in the sunlight a glass of rose wine like the clover in bloom, hand of the reaper, ah! if I had been able to hold you in my hands like a hunter so contented with the beast he long sought, you would soon be caught in the snare of words! But you rest no longer than an instant beside me on the already cut grass, a lively and sombre human presence, rest-less to yet take hold of and embrace everything that is bound to obey you.

Aimé's Slumber

The festival came undone like a bundle of wheat.

Oh! Louis, let's not leave yet. So sad to see, drunk with dance and cold wine, this crowd of harvesters suddenly abandoned by joy. They're losing their footing. One by one they start to drift away, groping their way outside themselves. One of them stumbles in a song with no way out, another knocks over a bitter glass. At the cry of a clarinet, the last polka cuts off.

Louis, how many times it's been dreamt of, this party that will die with the night! Remember. In the fields bitten by silent scythes, who among us, pulling from the shadows the pitcher of cider, arms sunburnt, who among us did not *see* the long tables of today beneath the trees? Let's not leave yet. Perhaps the musicians are only taking a break. And down there, the carousel continues to spin, with its gondolas, its lions and swans. Louis.

But Louis, who knows that a dying party is not to be revived, smiles, rises, goes. And Jeanne, and Rose, with a small sigh. Pierre awakens from this long desperate rage that for hours gives him a cruel face and curled lips. Beneath the tree where our horses await us, it's he who's crying now, his face hid in a dark mane.

Once again the joy has fled with the change of season at the very moment we were about to come upon it. They were to better welcome it, our dark clothes, our frocks with their beautiful silk belts, our frocks with their beautiful leather belts. In vain. Perhaps it does not like us to pursue it so. Farewell Hélène, farewell Pierre. Shall we try again?

Hélène calls us from over there without answering, with a lone finger she then puts to her lips. It's a man asleep. The carousel, that fells the space with an arm of light, an arm of shadow, lights up, darkens the youthful head against the branches. *Aimé*, says Louis softly, *It's Aimé. The whole week he was harvesting like a madman. Yesterday they brought back six hundred sheaves!* Pierre approaches, his hand extended, stops. Rose plucks a paper rose, leans, lets it drop.

He offered his hand to the night; the other sleeps next to the glass, freed from the scythe, freed from the razor-sharp straw of the bindings (those sheaves struggle under the knee like living bodies). He entered into his repose, it should be said, but that's how the dead are spoken of, and this heart beats more forcefully than ours. The dark breast slowly rises and falls; a silver chain trembles there; the neckline is glimmering. Sometimes as in the sky a great, pale, light-bearing cloud might be traced, upon his opened lips flowers a species of smile. Here we are, all immobile, our breaths one by one become prisoners of breath. Who will break the magic circle where the throes of the party expire like a froth?

Rose shivers, places her little hand in the large tawny hand left there and her mouth against an absent ear, patiently disputes with the shadow its human prey.

Gustave Roud

Tonight the man sharpens a scythe-blade on the grinding wheel turned by his son. His hands on the black and blue steel, his hands that I have been unable to portray (and the same silence paralyses me today), with their deep sudden cracks, their sharp ridges. Tawny hands, hands radiating their fleshy gold, an innate gold that light could not render more rich, since the light is incarnate in it.

I watch his hair where the silver already shows through, the start of the pure shoulder, right away covered over by the canvas. We speak, he laughs, raises his head again, and I feel the colour of his gaze where the light, there too, comes back to life.

Ah, who are you?

The stretch of sky between the column of pink bricks and the trunk of the aspen trembles with sparks like horses' coat beneath the flies of July.

Prairie's Powers

Who would think to question a vast and ordered land-scape's irresistible ascendancy, at once over our gaze and, piece by piece, over our being? It enslaves us gently, in the manner of a symphony. The sky, vacant or pasture to the clouds; the lands drawn out to their horizons with their naive features intact, or moulded by the hands of men, offer to the eye their grand themes, in no way bound to any temporal progression but pronounced across space in unison, where they forever secure the paradox of a simultaneous and immutable counterpoint. It is rather our vision that follows the length of each motionless phrase, enmeshed in the lace of shapely melody, the magic net, the relentless snare that every season, every day, nearly every hour bends, with the weight of so much fresh bait, beneath new harmonies. And the spirit eagerly suffers the delights of an expert capture: in an even-more startling paradox, these delights teach the spirit its most secret, most essential strengths. More than Amiel's celebrated remark, *every landscape is an emotion*, Brulard-Stendhal translates this mystery perfectly to my mind: *the landscapes drew their bows across my soul*, for this expression highlights the lasting likeness of landscape and lullaby.

A mysterious power plays indeed in the case of those grand, ordered spaces whose virtues surpass those of a mere soul-stirring bow to attain those of an immense orchestra, laying its plies from total silence to pure fury into a sheer universe of variegated inflections, and which, merely to interpret a few eternal themes, keeps at hand the sorcery of notes a thousandfold. A power still more mysterious in the case of an isolated fraction embedded in the larger landscape, whose welcoming gesture, by the secret virtue of a single clump of trees, of a liquid glint below a dark cluster of leaves, likewise draws us softly towards our finest self.

There I daydream, laying in a balmy October prairie where the encroaching evening spreads the ash and the oak trees' shade alongside me—a fleeting prairie, bounded by a screen of trees and a creek of little violence; one of those ennobling sites where the most rehearsed gesture, the most everyday thought, divested, as it were, of its contingency, reaches towards a simplicity serene and near to greatness. My friend and his cart, some weeks ago, were here loading the soft aftermath with which the wind delights to mix the mower's hair, or to cling to his scorched and naked shoulder. And this familiar labour, these always identical movements; the horses' halt, their advance; the pitch, the draw of the rake; the pitchfork empty, the pitchfork full and in full swing; it all unfolded against the dark and leafy backdrop like a sort of dance, steady and flawless, from which were banished any rhythmic misstep. Then like a rash of angry hives across the mown ground, the meadow saffron lit their tufts of flame. There was no one left. On Sunday, occasionally, the sound of laughter and brushing against leaves along the hedge: little girls were shaking the high hazel boughs. The grass grew green again, little by little, from one dew to the next. One morning, from up in the village, a herd hurtled down in a great tumult of cries and cowbells, immediately hushed. Only one shepherd led the herd, yet the beasts, their muzzles lowered to the chill forage, proceeded at an even pace, as though the strange calm of this place had dimly arrested them. I remember it. A rain as soft as mist began to descend; the boy, kneeling, was trying to coax a blaze from smoke beneath an enormous ruined umbrella as blue as his damp overalls. Already I could no longer hear the bells; they were themselves the thoughts they punctuated in perfect time, muffled or clear, and in the tempo of my step I also felt this tranquil cadence, as though recovered in it, and once again overhead, in the lovely sprays of branches dark against the sky in sequence. What is called plenitude is perhaps less abundance than concordance; it is a call and response, a *concert* in which each voice sings itself alone, yet nourished by the songs of others in its ear.

And poetry, which I had not dared to invoke for such a long time, was suddenly present as if it had obeyed some mysterious summons. Poetry, or a poet, rather. A lifeless stanza that had haunted me for hours sings suddenly in its fullest wealth and in the searing *reality* of its music:

> If *only*
> My *very courage does not expose me!*
> For *like morning air are the names*
> Since *Christ. Become dreams. Fall on the heart*
> Like *error, and killing, if one does not*
> Consider *what they are and understand. But*
> The *man's attentive pupils saw*
> The *face of God . . .*

I can *see* this Hölderlin, once he had taken leave, at the time of the hymns, from that which men call 'life'; Diotima dead, Schiller cruelly silent, I can see him plunging alone into his grand prophetic Night, where, as lord over time and space, poring over the 'immeasurable fable' of Earth and of humankind, he senses his imminent defeat, prepared to lose heart before the surge of presences conjured, gradually stronger than his expiring voice; casting ever-rarer lightning strokes across the centuries, and ceaselessly repeating this despondent

* Friedrich Hölderlin, *Selected Poems and Fragments* (Jeremy Adler and Michael Hamburger trans) (London: Penguin, 1998), pp. 247–9; translation modified to reflect Roud's translation into French.

cry to stave off the threat of silence: Ah! I *have so much, so much left to say!*—knowing full well he shall never say it.

My prairie listened then just as it listens now to this still-resounding lament. It even seems to me, at certain moments, that the prairie makes that lament its own, and grieves too, wherein each tree, each leaf, each clump of grass *signifies* in the face of an imminent winter that shall rob the prairie of its voice. Now the prairie too is alone, and like the poet, sovereign in its solitude. Before late autumn's final farewell, it rehearses its farewell daily, its welcome to the night. How may one abandon this place without secret affliction, as it sinks majestically into shadow, overrun little by little by the chill of hidden water; the green of the ash dwindling to ashes, their own high, blind bulk burdening the feeble daylight; while around them evening draws out and distils a sky forever more akin to crystal?

I loved the dark valley, the sound of water to my right, these pools of scent, unexplainable, that I crossed all at once. The headlights of a hidden automobile violently pulled the outline of a tree from obscurity, ripped trunks and still fronds from formlessness—touched the forest with a sort of haggard finger. Then they painted upon the embankment my shadow, stumbling, advancing, retreating by leaps and (I already heard this horse trot peopling the solitude) side by side with my shadow, fraternal, the shadow of a dragoon behind me, which dashed suddenly towards the slope, reached the top, immense, disproportionate, and leapt into the sky.

Difference

All that's left of the signpost is a mute shaft, but I readily recognized it, this vast crossroads that opened at the edge of the village. One of the roads descended between the houses towards a little low-lying inn: the *Star Café*. I remember. At the time I greatly feared the stars, and very nearly, having barely read the sign beneath the porch lamp, might have got back on the road. But the painted star was still better than her sisters teeming up above, that sharp wolf pack bent on piercing helpless prey, those executioners with lovely names ceaselessly resurrected, insulting Cassiopeia, fists outstretched in her burst of eternal laughter, Orion hunter once again, Hercules, Perseus—the spear, the lance, the hammer, all their bygone arms abandoned for one weapon alone: the whistling of pale, silent arrows straight to the heart.

I remember. At that time I would stammer every night, with this body vague and as if curled into itself, and yet stirred by a sort of excessively vivid and certain expectation, a word that is difficult to live with: *difference*. The paths of day are merciful towards these false vagabonds. For a swarm of stones, for women's laughter at the fountain, they give you a violet naked against your cheek, burst from the dead grass, and behind the hedge where the cold wind of late autumn is endlessly carded, this robin, always alone, who shyly turns towards you its gleaming eye, enclosed like a blackcurrant. But the shadow stripped me of named things. And I had no name. I went forth naked, my inner ear wide open to a bubbling of syllables, while up above, from one end of the sky to the other, the great luminous Creatures targeted their victim, disguising the hunt beneath a thousand fairy glimmers. I had no name. I did not know my name. Yet I sensed some obscure original baptism, a seal whose merciless signs I would one day spell out in the depths of my torn flesh. Laughable voyager! What a monstrous effort to conquer the mere threshold of the *Star*! And this voiceless voice towards the maid-statue leaning against the baluster of the gleaming bottles! I expected a burning upon the lips, the miserable flame that would descend bit by bit from the throat to the heart and here it was, the liquor fallen from these sleepy hands was nothing but a dubious opium perpetrating the worst of absences: being ousted from itself.

Ten, fifteen, twenty-five years. Twenty-six perhaps, and yet the memory of that quest and that halt rises up so powerfully here that, to say it, I involuntarily take up once again the solemn tone of adolescence. But today it's a man with grey temples who speaks. He knows his name. Against the asphalt, the cold wind of late autumn makes the dry leaves scrape, it chases the hail-bearing clouds, it enlightens my two empty hands. It caresses the riders' naked hair, lashes the manes' rough hair. It unleashes in the footsteps of the last runner, above and beyond the obstacles pallid in the daylight as dead as tombstones, the transparent leaping of a thousand frenzied beasts. It rushes under the fringe of eyelashes, as far as the impenetrable, the blue of this gaze that my friend calmly lays upon me.

For I am no longer the only one taking the path down towards the *Star*. Near me is the hand, higher than my shoulder, of my friend closed over the reins, and all these young men around us who I greet by name, and their horses numbered at the collar (whose difficult names I also know), all these voices, all this laughter gnawing blond locks, all these calls swept away like a swarm of leaves by the gale, and there all at once (the shadow has come) this lamp of yesteryear lighting up again above the threshold.

Enter! Push aside with both hands these shrubs of drinkers standing in smoke like an alder thicket gnawed by fog! The time is no longer for memories. Present our glasses to the silken girl who balances at the end of her arm the bell of pretty bright wine the colour of leaves! How our hands resemble one another! How easy it is to speak to men, how little then do they ask to recognize you! For I am one of you, am I not? Nothing unusual in my gestures—and you understand *everything* I am trying to say to you? To say that once at this same table an adolescent emptied false liquors to the yawning of a detached maid, ready to become once again the prey of the scintillating Sentinels until the dawn! Difference, O bitter poison of the soul and the blood! How many years traversing the seasons, voice unanswered and hands empty, with this fated companion, and the sole salute, at times, of a winter bird, the caress of a sole snowdrop flower! What an agony till the hour when the seal breaks at last, till resemblance at last attained, the cure! For I am cured, am I not? I resemble. I raise this glass with the expected gesture. I said the sentence rightly. I laughed, and no gaze turned away as it once did. You're getting up?

It's true, the ball is beginning. A single call of the brass instruments brought you to your feet before me all at once. You look at me without recognizing me, eyes adrift, mouth closed abruptly on an obscure sleeper's word. From the depths of your sudden absence you raise your hand towards mine. But here it is the same as all those hands of long ago that no one ever held out to me. Go. Do not even try to offer it to me, and what taste would it have on your lips, this wine poured by a *stranger*?

Leave me alone. A liquor, maid! and don't close the shutters yet. Don't light that lamp right away. It was reflecting itself in the windows, with all that festivity to which no one summoned me. It basely blinded the night. I blew it out. The shadow must see. Do you not know that the night leans at all windows, tireless, to find *its own* again, to take back, to call softly back, with a lone star barely murmured, those who claimed to be cured? The night must see me as I once was, hands empty, heart deserted, at this very table where for an hour I tried to escape it. It must forgive me. It must take me in at last for ever. I await the sign. I will wait for it until dawn if I must.

Cassiopeia at the heart of the highest window suddenly burns and trembles.

Under the thin shock of grasses there is the earth, they say, and more earth, peopled with rocks and roots, and further down the profound source of the springs, and then again the beds of rock one under the other, pleated and twisted like stone sheets, and the blaze begins where all things liquefy in the furnace. Truth some days perhaps, but not this evening: the road edged by two watery ruts is no longer more than a thin crust of earth between sky and sky. Whether the gaze rises, whether it sinks, the same constellations shine in the blackness of the liquid air. Lighten your load, voyager, slow your pace suspended between the double Lyre and the two Cassiopeiae. Do not run, for if you struck against an invisible stone, you would pierce with your body this ground that barely supports you, more delicate than the ice of ponds: you would plummet through the lower sky.

Do not stop either, if you do not wish to be caught up to the knees in the sand of the stars!

Of a Certain Purity

Should a man out for a walk, overtaken suddenly with joy, amuse himself by accompanying the rhythm of his steps with a little tune he whistles or sings, let him free to stretch along the countryside any melody he pleases: a show tune or a military march, a popular song pure or 'arranged' (according to Rimbaud's prophetic word), the remains of some symphony or sonata. But the musical phrase born from without, prose or poem, which emerges from among the whirling thoughts under the light wind of walking, which grows and coils into vines with each reverie, he himself cannot choose the line to sing, nor (as it would seem) can chance. It is mysteriously *dictated* to him.

So go these long walks in the fog of late autumn, not the brutal fog that turns the universe into a salvage yard, of wrecks appearing and disappearing in the same second, but the fog of half-mist where things, slowly separated from nothingness, relive a phantom life and then slip imperceptibly towards that fringe of non-being where they hesitate, where they still are and already are no longer, these long walks where vision and thought, imprisoned in a paradise of tenderness, become drunk on their own fragility, overwhelmed by delights in the infinite sparkling of nuance upon nuance—these walks each day brought a Mallarmé passage to my lips, not the invocation of fog from Azure, nor the 'dear mists' from the Pipe, but, inexplicably, a section from Un coup de dés, strict, scintillating, sharp, that announces the birth of a constellation:

   Except   *on high*   *perhaps as far as*
a place   *might fuse with beyond*   *outside*
the interest *as to that pointed out*   *in general* *along*
this obliquity through this declivity *of flames* *towards*
   it must be   *the Septentrion called* North
A CONSTELLATION *cold with forgetting and obsolescence*

  Inexplicably. Then I finally discovered what had dictated this fragment to me, even making it the unceasing companion of my course—it was the secret kinship of landscape and poem. That landscape made up of a sort of essential, sullen and wan absence out of which arose, only to vanish, a tree, then a hedge, a bird, then a man, a ploughed field, the plough, a horse . . . The poem made up of a different absence: the white of bare paper on which appear, marking great empty spaces according to the laws of one 'precise mental setting' (as Mallarmé himself puts it), words emergent one by one from a void that encloses them on every side, ready to dissolve back into it.

A landscape on the fringe of non-being. A poem on the borders of speech and silence.

*

The last roses in the frozen gardens, the ploughing interrupted, this morning I crossed a countryside of frost. It's winter. Here I am one last time standing close to the thresher, within the small bagging room. The sun is rising. It fires across the sky and against my shoulder a thick rose ray clumsy and tender as the hand of a friend. Beyond the threshold, the grass is frost. Under a hedge of frost, the stream no longer resembles that of *The Beautiful Miller's Daughter* but the frozen river of *Winter Journey*:

> In a pale and rigid skin
> River here you lie covered
> Icy body river stilled
> across the sands spread over
>
> With the sharp tip of a stone
> It is my dear loved one's name
> That I etch upon your ice
> The name the hour and the time
>
> Day of the very first words
> The day I was departing
> All round the name of numbers
> Twists and turns a broken ring.

But no. The water still runs raw and the poem flees with it. Another line takes form in the humming of the thresher, distinctly detaching from the noise and coming at last to live within me for some hours. They are once more the words of Mallarmé: a cry this time, long ago conveyed to the poor confidant Coppée (what does it matter?): *As for me, it's been two years since I committed the sin of seeing Dream in its ideal purity, whereas I should have been amassing between it and myself a mystery of music and oblivion. And now, having arrived at the awful image of a pure work, I have almost lost my senses and the meaning of the most familiar words.*

Why this passage? Ah! no need today to seek out the mystery of its origin for long. It leaps into view: the landscape before me, frost, sun, blank blue, reconstructs the very climate out of Mallarméan poetry. Its desolate purity calls forth an echo, silently, the 'pure work'. The bare trees, their sap dead (and already the gleaming of the frost at the tips of the boughs flow into steaming droplets), the barrier of rocks where the percolations of springs have frozen into murky chunks of ice veined like marble, all of a sudden something sharp: a sparkle of frost or the cry of a chickadee

Lost up above
With fury and silence

the water without a shiver, the dead straw at my feet amid the dead grass, I watch all of this, the space of beings and fixed things, little by little exchanging their customary life for another life: the pale life of signs in an air so empty and so pure that it becomes unbreathable. Space overrun by the *inhuman* whose insidious contagion spreads. It spreads insensibly over me, and the things within my reach. The handful drawn from the fountain of wheat becomes a sterile mass of grains, the sun on my shoulder pulls back its hand, leaves there the icy splinter of an astral light. The mouse scurrying without haste over the cobblestones, from one door to another, suddenly fleeing, outlines the skittish whirlwind of an abstract signature. It abandons ship, before it wrecks upon the shores of the absolute, since there indeed the brilliant ice floe of Ideas now rises before me—there where my eyes search feverishly for what gave it life—and recognizes nothing.

I lost my sense and the meaning of the most familiar words . . . The poet's complaint elicited by his youthful genius caught up in the vertigo of purity, it is not just today that it has come to live within me. All those former winters when I heard it resound inside me! All those nights amid the pure snow, the stars, the endless stairs whose every step signified the withdrawal of something, starkness, the man in his turn is made a sign! And the terror of returning, when it was necessary to return to life amid the other life, to outwit the name of each being, of each thing, to repeat it softly until it became *familiar* again! True captive of Mallarmé, I might have followed in his footsteps towards the illusory absolute of speech, through the mirage of a purity that could never be (and I did not know it then) but an inexorable return to silence. Yet one day I did discover that there was *another* purity, that of human innocence.

I was saved by a glance.

Near a low window (I had come there empty-handed, my head empty as a dawn sky with the glimmer of one last thought, my lips long forsaken by the most familiar words) the young man held upon his knee the beginning of a basket. A tuft of wicker was burning in the shadows. He was working without haste, his bare head leaning among the branches, his big tawny hands in such sure and simple movement that they wove in the air with the wicker a kind of silent music. I took a step. In my hands that no longer knew how to seize anything, I seized a willow branch, I *felt* it, supple and smooth. From lips that long since greeted nothing more than the most distant, the most forsaken stars, I tried to greet this man so close to me. He lifted his head, turned towards me a gaze in which lived all I had thought lost: the blue of the sky upon the August harvests, the blue of storm clouds, the blue of the spring which quenches the burning throat of harvesters before the water does, the blue of the sage made to be crushed in the hand of the reaper and severed by the scythe . . .

From the vertiginous borders of the other purity I fell at the feet of this man, still crushed from my whistling plummet through leagues of empty shadow, I was given back to what is human in me, I was slowly penetrating the purity of a being. A prisoner now of a *real* presence, guided to rest by the warm radiance of a nearby body and that series of gestures full of a calm certainty, I drank endlessly from the gaze heavy with welcome that had just opened up to me forever the magical realm of innocence. And this murmur that was already rising to my lips, indistinct, irrepressible, perhaps it was going to become song.

Like the insect beneath the bark or through the flesh of a fruit, the man burrows a tunnel into the fog with each step forward, a shifting tunnel behind him continually closing in. Should he come across another man, it is a miracle like that of two miners at the centre of their tunnels extending a hand to each other through an opening in the rock. With the same level of emotion as they have upon hearing, through the stone partition made each day thinner, the sound of an opposing pick-axe, I suddenly make out the striking of an axe in the cotton. A spot comes forth, something more grey than grey, a hardening of the fog: the human honeybee tucked into his cell of cinders. Aimé dismembers the cadaver of an apple tree; the sterile branches have already been severed and tossed into a heap beside the grey and rose trunk. We are alone, or encircled in a soft, formless Presence that grows sometimes heavy sometimes light, pierced by the rooster's call or the glimmer of a crimson facade—confused faceless aerial multitudes, comprised of vaporous eddies and sails that caress your face with a frozen fold. Already the pit is filled in: lawn put back clod by clod, like cobblestone. When spring comes, the scythe will glide effort-lessly over this space so long inhabited by the shadow, the fruit and the foliage. But the tree was old, the trunk shows a gaping hole where the birds had no trouble digging out a refuge. — And, says Aimé, this is not the only one condemned this winter. There are also the cherry trees at the hedges, just beyond. It's been too many years that they've been content to just stand there. —Yes, but what presence! (we would like to respond). They no longer bear fruit, yet how abundant the flowers in bunches upon the sagging branches, carrying, suspended among the corollas, bits of villages and forests! An absurd reply besides, for the 'every tree that has no fruit' suffers no reply, and these words, each man who pronounces them in his turn has the right to do so. He fears not this fog that holds you suspended in the void, isolating you from the world and yourself, uprooted, as all the reasons you have for carrying on break apart like dead branches in your hand. No pause for him in the long tress of tasks that the seasons have woven together for him like basket makers. With his heel he stamps the earth back in its place. He withdraws his hands from thick mittens of grey wool, he packs his pipe, lights it. So dark is the day that the flame rises in a beautiful rose gleam. He takes up a saw, tears from its teeth of blue steel a splinter that had wedged itself there. He speaks patiently, watches me, smiles. So many questions without vigour upon my lips! It's too late: a voice calls; it's supper-time. The mist, second by second, reabsorbs the great blue body leaving me behind.

The only password for four terrible months will be this crumpled daisy that I pick from the hollow at my heel.

Ancient November

In memory of Lieutenant Louis Ferrini

Night falls around six o'clock. We can walk for hours on end in the darkness; it's still warm out. The leaves beneath the trees glimmer in the mud. Like a swarm of bees, the stars have fled the leafy branches and ascended back to the sky. The nocturnal hive silently buzzes and burns. In vain. November is coming; another constellation rises into my gaze, endlessly reborn, triumphant even over the sunlight; the five lamps along one of the Olten bridges, years ago now, Ferrini—and you are at the hospital, in agony, you do not *want* to die.

Five lamps each holding like an unfailing note its fixed flame, beneath a most sullen sky, not because of the smoke from the factories, since they are closed, but because it is November, and the river, sullen indeed, also welcomes the five flames like a theme it distends and deforms endlessly according to the churning of its monotonous waters. Upon each bank are tufts of shrubs and trees the colour of night, and on the bridge perhaps, leaning his elbows on the damp ledge, a man lost in a

dead town where hour upon hour the step of the patrol-
men resounds, and he broods over an old poem that *sit-
uates* him, so much does he seem born of this very
countryside:

> The shadow of the trees in the misty river
> Dies like smoke
> In the air among the real boughs . . .

So long had we kept close to the tragic! I do not
mean that we did not participate in heart or mind, for
since the beginning of the war we could not not be
enlisted, and for our heart and mind the word 'border'
barely exists, thankfully, yet this word had materialized
for us with a singular and oppressive power. It was no
longer only an abstract separation, represented at most
by a few border points and Customs agents, that nothing
might suggest in the natural disposition of the country;
it was a very profound division, night and day, the end
of one world and the beginning of another. Here a tree
was still a tree, there a forest had become a confusion of
stumps half pulverized by lightning. Here a road, there
a ribbon softened by grasses beginning to grow back.
Here true clouds, there clouds like spontaneous vapours,
with a heart of rosy fire and a thunderclap piercing the
sky.

I can see once more that long month of January '08,
warm and humid, the village among the evergreens and
pastures divided by low crumbling walls that the snow

left in their shadow, encircled with a hard violet line. You were returning from the CDI, as it was called, a 'centre of divisional instruction' where a new training regime had been developed that you were assigned to teach, standing at the heart of a square course that had to be completed crawling, knees bent, what more do I know? Something inexorable that an obstacle course complicated and which left us broken, but ready too for the taste of afternoon's rest and that half-slumber when one follows, through one's lashes as though in a dream, a village girl guiding by their glistening reins two painted wooden horses. This is not the place to say anything more about it, and anyway who would feel touched by these things? But I would have liked at least to make the contrast felt between these first months of the year, their monotonous unfolding (February, was it anything else for us but the grouse frightened by a foot patrol somewhere between Les Verrières and L'Auberson or *Autumn Dream* reprised each night by a mechanical piano, amid the smoke and boredom of false liqueurs?) and those November days that came later, that were the last you ever saw, Ferrini, and so many along with you.

I look back at the road we have taken, the third day since the armistice. Two hundred metres from here, the long battalion column had reformed in the morning. What thoughts dwelt in it? The sort of stupor born of the hurried passing from the holidays, the lights, the bells of peace at last recovered (so it was believed) to the immediate reality of what could become a civil war and that began by the abandoned locomotives, the chrysanthemums tossed to you by anxious crowds, not daring to smile—the newspapers replaced by a square of soiled paper slightly larger than a plane-tree leaf. I am these troops that have left again, perpetually caught up to and overtaken by cars and overloaded trucks. They went down into the small town, set up for the night (they think) in the schoolhouse hastily bedded with straw, but there will be a train that evening; companies gather around the bundles; the unknown begins, with the shadow and songs where suppressed rage and also sadness resound.

There is nothing to tell, Ferrini. We're in a ghost town; at nightfall, the streets are deserted, more deserted still for the sound of a footstep whose count resounds suddenly beneath the covering of the old wooden bridge. On another bridge five lamps are lit; the river knots and unknots its reflections like long liquid locks of hair. A general strike breaks out, the army, as the *Rules of Service* demand, re-establishes order, that's all. There are sentries at the station; a corps of guards in the cinema vestibule; soldiers are eating in the dining hall of a truck factory. Everything is so calm now that our work is done: the people are happy, they are offering tea in small bedrooms lined with embroidered cushions ... Ferrini, ah! you're at the hospital, and every day more are brought to join you. Your terrible fevers, your rages, your deliriums, they are *recounted* to us. We have to leave without having seen you again. On the vast plaza along the lake to which we soon returned, the remainder of the troops falls to pieces: battalions made companies, companies made sections. Out of all those we have left, how many will they be when they return?

*

I went back to see the grave around which, how many years ago? we bid you a sort of farewell. And other graves as well (one perhaps recalls the list of the dead in the papers at that time)—but yours is the one that rests at the centre of my memory, and since it is up to me to break just once the silence where it lies, why would I leave already? Your grave sits by a small town lost in the plain where the willows hold each other's hands like children who, afraid of being alone, join hands and spin in jumbled rings out to the horizon. A town where there are also tall factory chimneys—but they have their own smoke—and a river too, less vast than the other one where we rested on the same November afternoon. *The shadow of the tree in the misty river* . . . The old poem shines once more with the five lamps, amid brass-band music, marching songs. And do you remember that other trip back, in March? It seemed that spring had stopped in its tracks and left along with us. We found a first lake again, the road followed still-bare vineyards. From town to town the air was milder that we drank in great mouthfuls, like a sweet cool liqueur. It's a stopping place within an orchard, by a chateau that lifts against the setting sun its towers of ash. You say nothing, holding in your teeth the first violet plucked from its nest of dead leaves.

'What if we returned?' one or another sometimes suggests, having in mind those places we crossed long ago. How can I respond? Are we the same? Are those places the same? To *what* would we return? To *whom* would we return? I don't know what madness caused me one day to question someone or other who came from there. At each person evoked: 'dead, dead.' It was always the same answer. Better still to be delivered defenceless to one's memory. If the throngs of shades, emboldened by the absence of swords, should drag you along with them, what does it matter? What could be more little by little alive than a shadow, for a shadow? At last, at the moment of leaving you at last, of asking your forgiveness for all this vain speech, of bidding you one last *farewell*, I feel with a sort of terror my words losing all their sense, and it is you who recalls to me in a low voice those words of a poet I have repeated for so long without quite daring to understand them: It is to live and to cease to live that are the imaginary *solutions. Existence is elsewhere.*

Near the grave—that I found again with so much trouble—
an aspen crackles in the autumn wind that carries back
upon a fleeting patch of sunlight the grey and yellow clouds.
A cross of rose chrysanthemums, lying on the marble gravel.
I thought there was a dead bee trapped within the petals, but
it is, touched by my finger—alive—one of those false bees that
haunt October gardens.

Not a single flower to toss there. Perhaps his parents are
still alive . . . search them out, write them—but what? One
man remembers, that's all. It's all so simple:

Died for his Country

Twenty-five years—it was yesterday. Others are now
living where we lived long ago, in the sombre countryside made
up of evergreens and pastures that the low crumbling walls,
where guns hang, crossed out with a shadow the colour of snow.
Another world . . . But the sun was at times so sweet that the
taste of our old life came back to our lips and we would stand
and say nothing. Then, in a leap straight upward, you were
already drawing with your sabre some fencing manoeuvre, and
my eyes in the binoculars, I began to contemplate once more,
confused, cradled by the yielding waves of a gulf of transparent
air, the dead forests of a land given over to the beasts.

You are near me, lips sealed. A life fulfilled, however
brutal that fulfilment may have been, how could it be thought
of with even a shadow of sadness? But perhaps you find that I
indeed resign myself readily indeed and that my friendship is
inconstant, for here a rosebush grown wild again touches my

arm as if to call me back to your grave. And, as I try to free myself, without understanding, it persists, and the sleeve of my jacket tears. Ah! my fleeting shadow upon your cross of chrysanthemums was lighter than a bee, but too heavy upon your slumber, because it is an earthly shadow—and who knows what shock came to disrupt your torpor, what lament you have tried, with all your strength, to hurl to me like a cry? Clumsy, like all the calls that those who lie outside of time elevate or murmur to those who still lie imprisoned within it. That is why I didn't know how to hear it. That is why the living never hear them.

Memory

An empty bottle, two glasses stained with rose among the ashes, the sparse light still muted under layers of smoke ... Just recently this glass was living on the lips of a man, this smoke wound around his breath, and the day as well drew before me with its living finger, out from the folds of the coarse jacket, bare-headed, the ammunition belt, the bare hands of a soldier who is my friend. Brief halt: a long ride was awaiting him before night to get to the squadron he had to rejoin, there where the valley spreads into plain spreads out, along a winter horizon, snow and clouds. *Farewell!* and already the hooves are clopping on the road. The rider heads out under the salt trees without looking back, alone with a song he sings, and the last walnut tree drapes upon the back of his neck the stinging scarf of its frost.

Farewell. It is no longer time to go down with you into the plains. The very straw on which you will sleep is refused to me. The registers at the inn and the stars, I know all too well what awaits me there, the dead trails, the black rivers amid the pale rotten snow. And all these things that your gaze, youthful and without memory, knows nothing of, all this *long ago upright in its terrible presence as soon as the city appears!* What will it be for you, this town, for your young laugh, your young blood given over to this anticipation of a moment that was ours as well, if not a promise of welcome at the threshold of night? But me, I know it well, I would not even see its bell towers, its lamps, its smoke—nothing but a stretch of marble and bare trees at its edge, among the prairies, where for twenty-five years thunders over a still-open tomb the triple blast of the rifles.

I know it well . . .

And yet, this young dead man (the smoke of salvos forever against the sky, blue on blue, the wailing of a fiancée forever in my ears, a dead leaf that passes through the prayer and comes to rest forever on the tip of a sabre with its shadow), is it he who would have called to me again tonight, if I had followed you? Would you not, with the simplest gesture: *your* finger suddenly pointing to an inn, to a star; with the simplest word: the town named by *your* voice, would you not have saved me from a memory? This gaping pit at the deepest place within me, would your mere presence not have closed it up again little by little? To both of us would you not have given us back *our* rest? You've left. But this room without you (leather, wool, wine emptied, cigar put out, the very scent of our Sundays past spent at the inns, the same patch of sun on the wall), memory triumphs here and now, and for a road that I have not dared go down with you, by a hundred steep paths, stirring up the cruel mirage of our resemblance, it chases me back to what I once was and what you *are*.

O the long night lasting for years become suddenly transparent! An ancient dawn rises in seamless purity over my lost youth, over a clutter of moments among places and seasons in chaos. Fanfares rip open a June morning; a winter sentinel bends his neck beneath the shower of stars. Annen ducks beneath the evergreens and grabs a warm blue dove spotted with blood. It has rained, all along the yellow road puddles splatter the horses' trotting. O the rainbow leaning there on the Ajoie, cool upon our eyelids like motionless wind. I have an Irish horse who's nearly unreachable, vast and deep like a ship, and who knows he has a poor rider. There he is galloping, sprung out of the line like an arrow far from the bow, and resounding the vain cries behind us in an irritated voice: *the thundering of Roud, the thundering of Roud!*

How he gallops, and how vain he is indeed, he too, his gallop in the sunlight without vigour of memory! By what miracle would he leap out of the past to join you, you who make your way down to a town, to a grave, with the *true* sunlight? With his murmured name, with your palm along his neck, you are stroking a dark living beast, but I, what have I been doing here for hours on end among the snares of time and absence, laughable summoner of shadows, a shadow myself in the kingdom of my dead.

*

I have fled these walls. I am sitting down by a patch of snow, beneath the ash trees of a stream, without a thought. My hand strokes the woollen leaves of a lungwort tuft. A new blue flowers suddenly on the living water. A blackbird hesitates, invents the first song in the world. The time of Farewell has passed. The time of Greeting begins.

Gustave Roud

Requiem

TRANSLATED BY ALEXANDER DICKOW

The perpetual grass gleams

<small>Maurice Chappaz</small>

Office for the Dead

No, not this single night's snow beneath the pale rose sun, where the bored gaze, from the skein of a thousand signs, unravels the feints, pursuits and famines of so many frozen beasts! What are they to me, these tracks too much like those of men? They all disappear into lair and blood.

Snow has other signs. Birds sometimes wound its purest shoulder with a single beat of the feather. I tremble before this seal of another world. Listen to me. My solitude is as perfect and pure as the snow. Wound it with the same wounds. A beating of the heart, a shadow, and this closed gaze will open again, perhaps, upon your *elsewhere*.

Come. No one is here. I am alone with the birds. I watch the water all scattered with dead leaves and foam. I watch the houses of men, those lovely villages upturned upon the hills like baskets of red apples,—all the villages I loved. Come. This one could welcome us yet, before the lamps. The doors are not all closed. One of those tall blue labourers that return with the mist up the paths strewn with straw and dead fruit will take pity on our quest and will come to know us. Our nightly dream must come to pass, that dream in which you always set forth again, all the way to prayer, all the way to words, on the terrible road of the dead. You speak to me. I listen with all my body without daring to answer a thing. You would like to leave, to find our lost home again, our nameless village. I obey. I rise. I set out again on a long walk, hourless and pathless in the grass, the labours, the snow. You forsake me no longer. You are here, at hand, O poor, timid presence, a voice, a wing, a shadow. You are no longer weary as you were long ago. It is you who now entreats me: rest yourself, rest!

But you know well that there is no rest.

Beyond the windows, yesterday, that onslaught of angels!

Their whiteness thickened in myriads darkened the sky with false shadows: a silent rush, a disarray of dead leaves, these bodies till the true night without end flung upon the fallen garden. And here they are, sleeping in the morning, featherweight wrestlers rolled in their great wing of scintillating salt, limbs already skewered with stems and live blossoms, snow of the absolute, killing field of frost, snow of signs too soon descended, melted into thick rain and keenly absorbed by roots in need . . .

Scatter yourselves without fear, extreme autumn asters, the time for farewells has not yet come! It is you who are called *harvesters* in my country, and you flower sometimes out of the dark when the wagons of young wine slowly crossing through the night brush against you, balancing from their casks the rosy flame of a lamp. You yourselves harvested, prey for the bees, high brume-blue shafts that I broke by the armful for a mirrorless room! And there awaited you, patient and resigned to its prison until the nuns' final *yes*, the lone bee of a gaze.

O with what harsh honey nourished! Living eyes separated from the immense hive of the world, your vain calls beyond the windowpanes towards the reflowered roses and the fiery autumn of orchards! Place of torture, O jail! Time and eternity at odds would strive against a torn flesh that sensed, thickening within itself each evening, the muted triumph of marble over blood. Time itself accepted its defeat, gently detaching your room from the river of the season like a boat heading towards its immobile shore. Upon walls already riddled with *elsewhere*, the signals of heaven and earth misplaced a last caress. The light, the night, were born ever further from your slumbers. But the shutters suddenly opening wide onto the pit of shadow and flickering lights, if I implored the stars for a less acute jubilation, Orion at the crest of the bare walnut tree always more present, more near, poured me in sole response a pale, poisoned honey.

Do you still remember? The sometimes-merciful pauses that would intervene and break this obsession over eternity, music, faces, and suddenly, upon the very sand of the absolute shore, time's last farewell . . . The light changes like a voice. It is no longer the helpless witness to an agony. It becomes sun again, this long living beam that kneels at the edge of the covers with wild, folded wings. You raise a hand. You offer him the worried hand that mothers slip onto the napes of their out-of-breath little boys. He takes the light in the hollow of his warm palms, gilds and stretches his fingers returning to their resting place. Your hands sleep in the shadow. Beyond, the first bee of the year grazes a windowpane and flees. A bee, a sunbeam, what farewell more delicate?

But already your ear is closed, and upon these sealed lips, absence draws the slow smile without an answer that will depart no more.

Between the blackened roses and these orange streaks of slime, nasturtiums just yesterday, an aster extends its stalks of ruffled blossoms, silently trembles, pleads! One distress for another, no abyss lies between that of plants and that of men. The absolute of a solitude draws them together to the point of exchange: I have lived this mutual pity. That is why I hear the barely muttered call off in the winter wind. I will go and touch the thin, frost-bitten stems, I will caress them just as they had long ago brushed their dying tuft against the shoulder of the tramp cast into dizzy nothingness of emptiness.

I will go—but what heavy presence regains this bygone bit by bit! The same liquor between hands inter-twined, the same scent caught in the curtains, extin-guished cigar, dust . . . What frailty binds me to this table? To send myself where, with a leaden step?

I will go—but already the tain of the night freezes onto the low windows. Each pane blinds me and afflicts me with a merciless double. Lost in the well of mirrors; entombed alive with myself. Alone. Innumerable. Alone.

Alone, never to have caressed nor culled the starry stem, more powerful than a golden bough, meant to open up our kingdom once again. Alone, and what pool of blood in the dark might ensnare the skittish Shade? Alone. A lamp flares, an hour resounds. Alone. The inn of the living is no longer that of the dead.

Upon the riverbanks one culls
sweet clover and viper's bugloss
The wet path circles all the hills
With a leaf-and-puddle necklace

The clouds the reeds and all the slow
grasses in long dishevelled locks
the sky and November willow
trees sink with water in the locks

The air tastes of the night's black frost
rent by a hunter's horn nearby
Preening its feathers a lone lost
bird with a sad piercing cry

No one can hear your cry Relent
Let your frail body rest instead
I *know* who calls me and laments
eyes closed to the sun of the dead

O this vigil, the final snare of the eternal that you set for me on the path to the ripe harvest! A single word in the blaze of noon, a cry sudden as an arrow—and the sky splits. All the power of *elsewhere* collapses upon the world, lashes a herd of frenzied hills, blackens and melts away the old gilt of the wheat, mows down the long lines of cherry trees obliquely and sweeps them into nothingness like the tatters of an extinguished celebration. Before me is no longer anything but a spot of *other* light in which I stumble and fall, dazzled.

Terrace beneath a great bell of light and the beating of these evermore urgent cries, as of a heart that chokes with the inflow of blood, succumbs,

my son my son my little one my son

brought low beneath this arc of calls from one edge of silence to the other

my son

one more time, at the edge of hearing, like a final beat
of the feather

then the voice stilled for ever.

I take an ever-slower step in the trail of signs that take flight at a single rustle of leaves. I tame the most furtive presences. I speak no longer, I ask no more questions, I listen. Who knows his true voice? As pure as it may come forth, the faintest echo of blood burdens it with muted menace. It is the man of silence that beasts alone tell apart from fear. Yesterday, a sweet, wounded doe took refuge just nigh to me, so calm that the killer's hounds howled in vain far from her lost scent. The morning birds weave and pierce a fine web of music with their beaks. A wren follows me from branch to branch at shoulder-height. I advance in peace. What does it matter if once again the prison of time has closed upon me? I know you will not call to me again. But you have chosen your messengers. The stray bird, the most hesitant star, the moth of souls, night and snow, that swarm about the old willows, to me everything is presence, cry; everything bears meaning. These hours that wilt one by one behind me like the bouquets thrown by children into the dust, I know that they blossom together in the limitless garden where you stoop forevermore. The swell of seasons intermingled pours at your feet like a wave the wheat, the rose, the pure snow. A Day made of a thousand days changes hue and shimmers at the mere beating of your memory. At last you *know*.

The ineffable. And yet, my soul defenceless, open to the faintest cry, I am still waiting.

II

Sometimes I walk back down towards the riverside copse of firs and ash trees where my life long ago received its secret wound of eternity. I recover a place without memory, absent and familiar all at once, and lavish with such a gentle welcome that I no longer dare question it, like a guest who stumbles over his words. Under the arc of alders, the stream fractures and confounds amid the drowned stones a whole foam of syllables; suddenly resumes with strange throaty laughter, shifts its voice and its reflections; doubles, in the mirror of a second, a pink stalk of fireweed; then distinctly articulates a phrase so nearly human that I wear myself out trying to capture it, while at my shoulder crackles a tiny rain of needles and bark, a squirrel's greeting from above.

Vain returns, and of all of them, today's perhaps the most vain. But the road had to be taken again. I couldn't,

I can no longer bear trying to define this mystery within myself into which everything inexorably buries me again. You know it: at the centre of my life, there is this fault line, this transparency, this indescribable lapse to which my gaze and my thought affix themselves, fascinated. One day I was admitted alive into eternity.

In this very place, in this innocent space of flowing waters, of foliage and of birds so readily becalmed. The eternal is not a Promised Land at the extreme end of a pathway of sweat and tears, and none could force an entry into it by some fraudulent intrusion, since we are *within it*. The knowledge of it that a grace may grant us is as brutal as a rapt. *It* enters into us with a fundamental, irrepressible quaking of the being; our blindness is torn from us at once, like the leucoma from an eye that has run dry. That of the body, that of the heart, and the voice of our dead then immediately arise in an ample and sudden plenitude. No longer your former frightened calls, always nearer to silence, but the triumphal hymn mysteriously granted to that of the blood, this blood that I hear and *see* flowing like a mystic sap in the world's every vein.

Yes, I have been this man traversed. My fingers knotted around the narrow trunk of an adolescent ash tree (I can still feel the smooth coolness against my palms), with my whole body I have sustained eternity bursting out, I have suffered the assault of the ineffable, I have seen the true light, the same one, wash over all these transient things around me, infusing them with the splendour of a symphony . . .

Since then, a silent *nevermore* has slowly taken possession of the site. At each return, I felt time on the lookout there, taking care to avenge its fleeting defeat by multiplying its mirages, eluding with a thousand ruses the only questions that always return to my lips: 'Who desired it, why?' At its command, everything has returned to its most quotidian resemblance and maintains it flawlessly, everything, up to the wood-dove's stray feather, up to the shadow of hair grass on the path. But hope is stubborn and credulous. It is hope which, through so many years, has not stopped bringing me back here on a quest without answers. It tears me from dismay, it declares beings and things innocent of their naive subterfuge. *Time forces them to lie*, it whispers to me, *they imitate forgetfulness, but you feel it, they too remember that light; do not abandon them!*

I obey. I return to the foot of the ash tree of long ago. I greet the large trunk, the crown of delicate leaves and titmice. Yet another time I gently caress the bark with its deep cracks, striped with moss and lichen. And I keep watch in vain for hours upon the column that would be more insensible than death, for the merciful appearance of a sign, of a memory, of the reflection of a reflection, a touch of sun that's a bit too bright, the spot of gold that the shadow would not efface.

October . . . But have the months kept their names for you? At night, the cold wind pursues an icy moon to the slopes of the sky and on the earth the first drifting leaves. In the morning, they are found pressed against the threshold. Strange presents of the dawn! There is sometimes a dead and bloodied mouse, a few feathers, seeds fallen from untouched grape bunches in which the blackbird forages with its beak, wings aflutter. Herds of bells suffocate in the fog. Is it the fog too that stifles your voice, mine? Who am I to speak to, if you no longer hear me? Life has walled men in like the most exact of tombs, that deaf people, their ears rent by their own blood! And you know *who* led me as far from them as this forsaken region; you know the cries, the farewell, the tears drunk in the sands of the desert inside . . . Each night, each day I make it alive to that frontier of time, but that no one passes before his last heartbeat, sheet of snow broken through with each step, always thinner, its extreme fringe at last melted into that bank of fog or absence that is *Elsewhere*.

Deliver me from my secret, you *must* hear me. Ah! how to live thus between two worlds, torn between them without reprieve? And light, my last resort, has betrayed me. Once faithful, swift to answer the slightest glance seeking the hour, the season, daybreak, scarcely now has it followed me to the confines of time than it denies it with the furious liberty of a slave unchained. It blazes up, it dies down, then hollows out of the new shadows around me dazzling grottos in which my dead welcome, with a single bat of the eyelashes, recovered clarity, finishing without haste their interrupted gesture. All present, with an inexpressible presence—and you alone awaited in vain. Ah! perhaps there is another *elsewhere* to which you escape, displeased with my fleeting access to the eternal. Forgive me. It is you alone that I call to, you alone, you know it.

October . . . The tattered mist has fled, the sun slightly warms a hedge of soft ash-green. Only the highest leaves yield to the cold wind, float for an instant in back of the sky, then, crackling, rejoin their shadow among the grass and the bare flesh of the autumn crocus. A labourer advances along the stubble; his pace marks the time in the thick earth, marks human time, and the light follows the team like a humble maid with golden hands. She stops when the boy, standing at the end of the furrow, recalls his horses to the line and tips over the ploughshare in a flash of steel. She caresses the tuft of daisies sliced at the feet of the young body, a shoulder, one pure arm . . . And the voice once again sounds like a call, alive and tender. The only voice that reaches you there in the truth of its flesh and blood, more powerful than death. Perhaps you heard it already; perhaps, seized in hearing it with an obscure regret for the transient, you have set out again on the road without measure, drunk from drinking again at the source of the instant ; perhaps you are here among us; perhaps, and you tremble, O presence more vulnerable, more fragile than a leaf . . .

III

This dwelling I no longer have the strength to care for
sinks into weeds, surreptitiously, the stones of the walls
pulled free, a blind moss upon each shingle, at the heart
of the garden that grows wild irremediably . . . One by
one, the worn-out plants collapse beneath nettle and
thistle; the mauve clematis is dead. Ah! may you know
nothing of this agony. How will we be able to live in a
here grown unrecognizable?

Saddest of all: that pity of beings and objects that
would like to support us still, from all around. The fountain, night and day, where the last horses come to
drink—and their charitable masters bring our barn back
to life for a time by stuffing it with ripe wheat. The harvester farmhands no longer plunge into the pools their
burnt arms, but the water whispers or sings unfaltering.
It still seeks, in the hollow rooms, the ear of vanished
sleepers, as if to slip its secrets inside at all costs, all that

it knows of the earth's innards, those regions of sand, shadow and rock where oozes and forms drop by drop its deep source. Who henceforth will hear it murmur at the edge of its summer dreams, their fever vanquished by its coolness?

Everything here is beginning to doubt itself, anxiously scrutinizing its very being, evermore threatened. The great constellations are grazing and trampling in circles above the night's roof of black grass, glittering but gradually forgetful of their names, flickering on the very edge of absence. And the dawn wind that you loved, frequent visitor of the flowering linden, of the sleeping roses, vainly pours upon the unwelcoming facades its slow libations of aroma.

O our turmoil! Like a sheaf, its bond broken, ceases to be a sheaf and is denied in each of its scattered ears, this ravaged place falls back into the uncertain and draws us along with it in its dizziness.

Space itself is no longer secure.

Gustave Roud

(No, it is not the present distraught dwelling, yielding beneath its burden of solitude, it is the other which awaits us, the other. O birthplace! Like a patch of snow at night, its walls gleam gently behind a mesh of boughs and years, in the depths of time, among the dizzying prairies of childhood. So vast that no voice could have reached the reapers at the fringe of the domain when, noon being near and all the dew drunk, even beneath the dome of the orchards, they pricked up their ears, impatient for a set table, with soup and fat slices of grey and pink lard. But someone at last was hailing them from afar at full horn-blast and the invitation rolled for a long time through the expanse like a dull chain of sounds without echo.

Against the present wall, suspended on a wool cord, that hollow horn veined and smooth, a patch of light at the embouchure, one hundred times I have grasped it, put it to my lips, taken it from them again. Its calls once traversed space; today it is time, still impure, that they would have to vanquish. There is no cheating time. Bring it back to life with my breath? Half-awaken the former scythe carriers? What turmoil, what terrors would seize those nearly blind shades, lost far from the path among the high grasses or still caught up to the knee in a pool of nothingness!

O mother, keep me from that cruel game, that I may one day cross the threshold without fraud.)

But the infinite loyalty of birds . . .

From childhood, the kingdom of their song and flight open like a merciful refuge! The deserts of a voiceless soul suddenly peopled with their voices, the poet redeemed of his silence, when the larks' jubilation moves the sky to its peak. A sole blackbird in the still-naked hedge erased winter. And let a warbler sing at dawn, drunk, beneath the June showers, the black court's clerk of daybreak, our executioner, straight away cease its demands, its torture, dissolve and flow into the shadow.

Their loyalty, their familiarity, their delicate pity! And their distress, sometimes, profound sister of your own. It is that distress that makes of them your messengers, our guides, always quick to take over your long, exhausted signals. I did not know right away how to hear you: no one can without having seen the slow settling of his sadness. But as soon as a transparency is found again, what a jolt when the bullfinch in the October grove, a pink flame among the ash trees' blackened leaves, cast its call to me, that lament—your own, indubitably—that consoles and tears apart a heart hardly resigned to farewells!

How you loved them! Recall the robin encircled with snow, in the depths of time, long ago, in the forsaken garden, its anxiety behind the windowpane with its pale ferns of frost, the strange tree where it was nesting, that dome of needles impenetrable to the freeze, and its forgotten name, more strange still.

Will they one day rise up again from the temporal abyss, those buried syllables? Will the *forever gone* of your voice now silent be undone?

Unremittingly, every day, I question.

Swallow, discoverer of spaces, weightless body beneath the long feathers of bluish steel, a stain of immemorial blood upon your breast, each morning, from your wire perch covered in verdigris, you were tearing along furiously, shrill, brushing, denouncing, driving out the cat's false sleep among the curly hyacinths, and the rite accomplished, rose again to your song, evermore taut, more talkative. Companion endlessly listened to, contemplated endlessly, opening, refolding one wing, then the other, with alternating winks and that crackling of the throat before each pause of the voice, oh so like your sisters wheeling up there, so ready to meet them in the sky's fullness that our brotherhood seemed to me to be born each day from a new miracle . . .

I did not hear the timid call arisen little by little from your mere loyalty of presence, I did not know our meetings to be prearranged nor why you fell off abruptly in anguish at the very heart of exultation. And you, all full of your secret, dying to confide it to me, the fervour, the stubbornness, the anger, the despair fed your song to the breaking point. You were trembling, near to a trance, and I saw your breast beat, beat under the half-open beak.

Ah! what can a little bird do against the old deafness of men? Yes, they spell out the wood pigeons' cooing or the blackbird's exercises, one evening at the bottom of the April sky, but only to lose their breath at the first lark. In my turn, I tried to follow note by note, breathless, those passionate outbursts, as one sometimes hears roll out from the lips of sleepers a flood of obscure words. Beyond the song, through it, I felt it: things were being relentlessly said in which we would finally learn our deep powers. But something in me remained closed to that language. Excluded from the marvel and the secret, crippled with waiting, tottering like a treasure hunter with empty hands . . .

O the sadness of returning by the paths of the fields, the last lark fallen back to the stubble, beneath the vault in which it is already shining, the deadly ambush of the Sentinels!

Your cries, your songs . . . He who strains and exerts himself to decipher them, freshly arisen, persists in vain: I have suffered the cruel lesson, led for years that pursuit ever ready to founder before the *no* of an impossible exchange.

But in the very time when the swallow's song at the edge of morning was dwindling ceaselessly, eaten away by the imminence of failure and reverted little by little to that poor, stammering prayer, in the most obscure region of being the light of a muted certainty, O unhoped-for birth, was awakening like an answer to the defeat of want and desire.

A truth has arisen in me, the same as that paleness of the horizon when the dawn from shadow without violence frees the face and the hands of the nocturnal walker, and gently loosens his knotted throat. Everything that the birds *wanted* to say to me and that I let flee, so I thought, just as the clumsy winnower throws his seed to the wind with the chaff and the husks, everything is saved, everything found its way to the heart, that crucible in which their millions of calls melt at last into the gold of a single voice. I hear that hymn well up in me, each inflection persuasive above and beyond any word—strangely familiar, too. For it is you, yes, I recognize you: vanished, but closer yet than during the summer months, little outspoken sister. Your nests are empty, those airy boats of hay and mud moored on the rafters of the jutting roof; you had little by little returned to silence: no more screaming hunts at dusk, fled the swarms of golden midges! Barely a bit of anxious twittering before immensely taking flight.

Gustave Roud

... Our anxious twittering, yes, and this great stirring of wings: we sensed the moment of taking flight; soon space would take on its transparency. It sometimes delays, is muffled with fog at dawn and patches of cloud, at night, disorient the sky. Where may we read our route in this confusion of stars?

—How I have lived through it, your fretful expectation in the dusks of late summer, when the young harrower, head and hand lifted, joylessly pointed out your rounds to me, your rounds above, feverish to the point of dizziness!

—And me, *from the sky, I suddenly took both your faces in a loop of flight, to lose them, to regain them straight away ... But the grand night of departure! Our beating feathers ruffling the air like silk, each beat of my wings lightened by this burden of memories and images: the nest above the fountain,* bristling with little wide-open beaks, our long apprenticeship, that secret also that had to belong to you at last!

—It belongs to me, yes, but with such gravity (and as if veiled) that its approach intimidates me still.

Listen, I have sometimes kept watch until dawn upon the harvested hill. I endlessly questioned the pure space in which still rustled, imperceptibly, the flight of your invisible swarms. Little by little the soul, strangely, was opened to these star-studded depths and seemed to receive them in itself to the point of reaching their magnitude. Dumbstruck, deserted by brief moments of sleep, I felt this invasion of the expanse evermore intensely. And the moment came (you *must* believe me) when, as far away as the goal of your flight may have appeared to me, I glimpsed it *within myself*, as if I contained the world. There was no, there would no longer be any *elsewhere*.

—*At last, the threshold of the secret crossed! Quickly, before the vision abandons you, learn thus of your power! Prolong your inescapable waiting no longer, close your eyes, contemplate, feel your deep inner reality: those great temporal spaces linked by a transparency that love alone can perfect. This achieved, and the priceless reuniting shall be given to you. Yes, you contain the world; there is no more* elsewhere *for you in the expanse. There will no longer be one at the heart of time if you take time on also and surround it within you for an ultimate decantation. And she who had fallen silent, as if seized again by the wave of an infrangible sleep more powerful than your two hearts, it is she with whom you shall reunite at last.*

—Shall I have some hour to prefer, some site?

—Find one of those places where a second's illumination once revealed you to yourself and tied thereby to this landscape of welcome, evermore brotherly, up to its softest hill, its most humble cluster of flowers.

—Yes, I will know how to choose it, to stretch myself out, to close my eyes ... But that inner reuniting that you announce to me mercifully, I tremble to sense it so close. Ah! I dream of a pure presence, of a youthful intercessor, of a brother in grief at my side, and we would go together towards the promised meeting, each traversing his own transparency, to reach at last that light that awakens also in each of us, but where *everyone* finds themselves.

The gaze of the labourer who was showing me in the sky of his village your fretful wheeling was blurred with tears and I did not dare ask him the reason why of his sadness, but his lips suddenly unsealed, he murmured the name of a young dead woman, his voice soon broken by those difficult sobs of men in which the whole being is torn apart.

Ah! to run to him, to take him by the hand, to bring him without saying a word to the edge of the ploughing, in the grass blossoming again; to wait together (on our lips the name of she whom we have lost) for the way to open within us.

O mother, it's the end of those questions brooded over across the years, in the wear and tear of all resignation, like an herb of bitterness.

O mother, a bird has given me the *sole* answer. From grief to grief, it took a whole life, my whole life to receive at last this gift undeserved: the secret that will join us.

O mother, listen: there is no more *elsewhere*.

The labourer stretched out near me, his eyes closed, the dark fringe of eyelashes still moist—but at the hands of the light his youthful face has regained its gentleness. The disorder of features gives way to the impalpable caress, the breath lightens, the fits of the heart are calmed. The pure chest rises and falls without haste; it uncovers, hides, uncovers at the foot of the gleaming golden straw a pool of sky: the bunch of cornflowers saved from the ploughshare by a miracle . . . O brother, your hand clenched upon my own gives way; heat, blood are returned to it. I feel it and only barely feel it any more, as at the moment of a farewell, a presence still, but weakening. For you are growing more distant, immobile; beneath your eyelids are already blooming the images of time crossed back over; you precede me in transparency.

Or will I remain prisoner of the instant and the site?

But like a brotherly answer, you smile, sleeper so close, your smile is that of one who did not dare to hope and who suddenly sees the fulfilment of his hopes. It is born upon your lips like the dazzled announcement of your reuniting. I know it: now it will be my turn to traverse these spaces immediately open to your innocence, as pure as the sky of the migrating birds. The country around us, which was sinking towards evening in a glory warmer and more golden with every minute, is seized by another light today, dully infused in the expanse, fixed, pale like translucent milk. Oh! I recognize it, that September brilliance ever gentler and more bold. It both caresses and freezes. It interrupts the mobile exchange of forms and shadows. All is isolated, stripped down, drawn further into itself; all recovers the gravity, the peace of an immutable presence at the heart of the absolute crystal. A blank light like a toneless voice, I no longer hear anything but it, prisoner perhaps of a mirage without duration.

No, the swallow did not lie. The long chain of blues that carried my thought out to the horizon is burst and scattered: lovely shadows the colour of lavender upon the dust of the road, smoke from the field-burning and smoke that crowns the dark rose of a forsaken village, the peaks beyond at the edge of the sky, a scattering of gentian, and the sky itself, beneath the slow eyelid of the clouds, like a gaze . . . I see them grow pale, dissolve bit by bit (and your body itself) in the expanse, like the clouds that blur the stars before the night the birds take flight: a vapour, a mist yet, then the inexpressible advent of transparency. The azure of the spared cornflowers alone, strangely, is brightened at the threshold of the abyss of pure time and space, patch of sky, soon a gleam, beneath my closed eyelids, of such a tender blue that it stirs the soul like an innumerable summons.

Already (but this word outside of time just died) from the most faraway region of the chasm an echo struggles to answer, more fragile than a young sprout out of the loam of silence, in the light of eternity.

A patch of sky

a sky-coloured patch

> the deep blue of corollas in a crown

I lean down, reach out a hand: no cornflower, my God, but the flowers whose reflection I have sought all my life in the gaze of men . . . Ah! here they are again, those small Apennine anemones, patches of azure, long ago, cluster of stars from out of the leaves in a feathery muddle, in the shade, beneath the rowan of our garden, O mother, beneath the rowan of the Garden.

Kneeling once more before them, welcomed again by the world of flowers that having hardly left the cradle I discovered, babbling with joy, at the edge of the multi-coloured baskets, in the scent of crushed grass, visited in turn by a procession of perfumes...They are revived, they bathe my neck once more; each breeze descended from the peaks gathers them again and brings them to me, having brushed against the jasmine, the bitter box-wood and the lilacs. They revive space in turn, and the facade that appeared is calling me with its gleam like a long snow's song. The pine is reborn on the lawn strewn with its cones, with the old dying plum trees. O these presences around me who rise and recompose, in the fever and the peace, the *all*-presence, as though to heal this place of its wound of infinite waiting! There, the blue valet stops, draws with his rake, out of the sky, a sus-pended bunch of cherries, and the lovely grass-snake at his feet twists and flees in a quiver of tall grasses.

I acknowledge, I know all things, myself acknowledged, greeted, in the light where the robin plays, orange and grey like a false dead leaf. He approaches, retreats towards his tree renamed, returns, follows me, encircles me, accompanies me with flight and song (that ceaselessly picked bunch of prayer and laughter) up to the old worn threshold between its rosebay bushes, the threshold of reuniting, O mother, where all words, in the ineffable brightness, come undone like a vain foam.